STARGAMES

STEALING THE SUN: BOOK 7

RON COLLINS

SKYFOX
PUBLISHING
Science Fiction

STARGAMES

STEALING THE SUN: BOOK 7

Cover Design: © Ron Collins

Cover Image
© Philcold Dreamstime.com

Skyfox Publishing

ISBN-10: 1-946176-34-6
ISBN-13: 978-1-946176-34-9

STEALING THE SUN

includes

STARFLIGHT

STARBURST

STARFALL

STARCLASH

STARBOUND

STARCRASH

STARGAMES

STARDUST

STARBORN

Other Work by Ron Collins

Wakers

The Knight Deception

A Trevin Knight Thriller

Saga of the God-Touched Mage

includes

Glamour of the God-Touched
Target of the Orders
Trail of the Torean
Gathering of the God-Touched
Pawn of the Planewalker
Changing of the Guard
Lord of the Freeborn
Lords of Existence

Picasso's Cat & Other Stories

Five Magics

Seven Days in May

Tomorrow in All the Worlds

Follow Ron at:
http://www.typosphere.com
Twitter: @roncollins13

For Mom

I miss you

CONTENTS

INTRODUCTION

I should just simplify everything and paste my introduction to STARCRASH here. That would be cleaner, anyway — though I suppose I'd have to adjust a little here and there to update book numbers. Such is life. There is no easy way out.

So, let's see — just where is that "Copy and Paste" function when you need it?

The last time I sat down to write one of these introductions, I laid out a story of woe about how I had been tricked by my own work, and how I first thought this story was six books but had finally given in to the fact of the matter that, no, it was seven books.

Joke's on me.

Turns out *Stealing the Sun* will be not seven books, nor even eight. It will be nine.

I'm pretty sure of that, anyway.

I know how it ends, so that's a point in my favor.

I suppose it's only fair that this storyline sprawled out from under my thumb. That's the nature of life after all, the nature of people and our communities to be unpredictable. It seems only natural that things have taken paths different from what I first expected.

That's my excuse anyway, and it sounds good on paper. So, I'm going with it.

I suppose I should also talk about the gap here.

If you've been reading this series for any time, you know what I mean. It's been a while since STARCRASH was published, and that was, of course, not the plan.

Life has interrupted, though, in a plethora of ways that I'll not completely bore you with here but that wandered through a myriad of health problems in the family, the pandemic, and a few other sundry items. You each had your own set of problems over the past few years, however, so let's not dwell on these things.

Instead let's look to the future.

Or at least the now.

As I was finally writing this book a few things became clear.

It was going to be messy in the way that complex things are messy. There's a war of sorts going on, after all, and if there's anything you learn when you look at the way wars play out, it's that so much of war's result comes about through random luck, or because of things done by those invisible people on the front or in the trenches, or someone just trying to get on with their lives. This book has a lot of that going on.

I wanted to capture that.

I think there's a lot of that going on in the real world today, a lot of everyone's everyday life influencing things around them, and each of those things seeming more and more likely to change someone else's world.

I also realized the book was going to be intricate to put together, delicate in a sense, because it had moving parts and all those parts had to play together in the end. This is something I'm enjoying about writing this series though. Interleaving stories across an entire galaxy of existence is complicated, but intriguing and satisfying in the same way putting together a jigsaw puzzle is. I didn't want to lose anybody in the process. The characters had to be real. I was going to have to spend serious time in each of their points of view.

Which of course is part of the fun of being a writer.

Oh, woe is me.

Did I succeed?

Will the story touch you? Will it deliver you to the following book ready to dig in even further? Did what I accomplished matter?

Everyone who reads this may answer those questions differently.

But for me this book has made a difference. This is my transition book. The book I wrote as I was coming out of the morass of the past couple of years, and looking into a hopefully brighter future.

With luck that future will include finishing a NINE book series.

Fingers crossed.

Ron Collins
April 2022

NEWS

SOURCE: INFOWAVE — NEWS for the 23rd century
TRANSMITTED: June 20, 2252, Earth Standard
HEADLINE: Top Scientist Pentabill Dead, Ambassador Black Missing

Florecer — Emil "Oscar" Pentabill, one of the system's premier wormhole scientists and a key contributor to work that led to Star Drive technology, died today under uncertain circumstances. The scientist fell from the balcony of his high-rise hotel room after attending programming at the Galactic Council on Wormhole Physics, a gathering of the system's biggest scientific names.

One of those names was United Government Science Ambassador Torrance Black, an acclaimed hero of the Everguard attack, who is now being reported as missing.

Authorities have made no official statements about the death or the disappearance except to say that every effort is being made to learn the whereabouts of the science ambassador. People inside the investigation, however, have suggested that the case is being pursued as a homicide, and that Black could be considered a person of interest.

Pentabill, who was eighty-eight standards old at the time of his death, leaves behind a wife and three children.

SOURCE: INFOWAVE — NEWS for the 23rd century
TRANSMITTED: June 21, 2252, Earth Standard
HEADLINE: Pentabill Linked to Universe Three

Reports are circulating that Emil "Oscar" Pentabill, recently found dead on Florecer after falling from a hotel room balcony, was directly connected to the terrorist group Universe Three.

Longtime friends of Pentabill have said that the scientist was a collaborator with Jorge Catazara, a professor of wormhole physics who defected to U3 years ago, but until now Pentabill had not been connected to the defector in any official way. Inside sources are now saying that United Government intelligence agencies have known Pentabill was sharing highly classified scientific data with U3 operatives for some time.

These same reports suggest that investigators are trying to find out if the terrorist group was involved in Pentabill's death.

"Pentabill was planning to reveal where U3 had embedded key agents inside the Solar System," an anonymous contact said. "It's likely they killed him to keep their assets safe."

In related news, authorities have issued rewards for information that would lead to finding United Government Science Ambassador Torrance Black, who has not been seen since the attack that killed Pentabill. Evan Abade, a spokesperson for the investigation, declined to make any direct accusation of Black, but did suggest that their team is looking forward to an opportunity to speak with him.

"The more time that passes, the more concerned we are that something nefarious has occurred," Abade said.

The spokesperson refused to speculate on what that nefarious event could be, responding only that "it would be a poor investigation that ruled anything out. We're exploring every idea at this point."

Any person who has information that might help the investigation is encouraged to come forward.

INTERVIEW

CHAPTER 1

Location: Arlington, Virginia
Local Date: June 30, 2252
Local Time: 1643

"Feel free to have a seat and get comfortable," the towering assistant said as he gave Zina Nichols access into the office. "Director Pinot will be here shortly."

The door closed behind her, and Zina, already sensing the taste of power in the room, paused to nervously adjust her vest, gently shaking her arms to relax before entering farther. The sleeves of her dress jacket came comfortably to her wrists, covering her body art. The director wouldn't care about the patterns there — just the opposite, in fact. But she wanted Pinot focused on things beyond her body art, so she had chosen the outfit to keep him from admiring them.

Zina had gotten this rare slot on Pinot's calendar by being sharp with her work, and by doing a series of favors for his assistant. It was only fifteen minutes, and it was late in the day, but she was prepared. She could get a lot done in fifteen minutes.

The setting had been the director's choice.

She assumed he had chosen it for his own comfort rather than any other purpose, but she was happy to be here rather than in the conference room next door — which was an elite place that hosted the director's more social gatherings. She thought he might have chosen that location simply to flex his muscles, to show off its view — which given its reputation would be quite intimidating, a tenth-floor scan of the Potomac displayed through floor-to-ceiling glass panels.

That room would reek of power.

Elite brokers would make their elite decisions in a room like that.

She could already feel the separation from reality inherent in that room, though, a sense of certainty that comes from being so far removed from the consequences of those decisions.

This office was better.

There was strength here, too, but a different kind of strength. A strength that came from precision and an intense attention to detail.

The air here was intimate.

It made her more confident.

Willim Pinot, director of the United Government Intelligence Office, and her boss's boss several times removed, was a man who thought hard about things no one else even knew existed.

The office was longer than it was wide, sparely decorated, but comfortable. Its sense of perspective made walking the path to take one of the two guest chairs — both angled perfectly to focus on the director's throne — feel like she was traversing a tunnel.

The desk, positioned at the exact center of the wall, was made of carbon composite, polished to a dark shine.

The flag of the agency draped from a stand behind and to the left of the desk — real fabric rather than the simple wall displays so many other officers chose to fly.

She was certainly being observed, so she fought the urge to examine the collection of photo plates mounted at fashionable places along the wall. The photos called to her, though. She had studied Pinot for years — starting with a paper she'd written in high school. She admired that the director had come from the lowest ranks of analysts to make his way — or cut his way — to a position where the world's most connected people could consider him the most powerful man in the universe.

The pictures made her flash to a memory of a late-night study session with a handful of classmates. They had all had too much fruity gin to drink, but she recalled debating a remarkably assholey classmate over whether Pinot *was* the United Government Intelligence Office.

She gave an involuntary chuff at the memory.

He wasn't the first to underrate her and wouldn't be the last.

Being dismissed, or overlooked and ignored, came with being "dainty," as her mother had called her, or "a skinny runt" as her brother had. And she *was* small — a hundred fifty-five centimeters, or just over five feet tall. And thin — she would top a hundred pounds only after a big meal. Her study of martial arts gave her a different perspective, though. Zina Nichols had long ago learned that her petite stature — and her sometimes awkward need to think through things before she spoke — could be put to her advantage, that she could leverage her opponent's momentum to dislodge them.

Whatever happened to that idiot, she thought.

Not that it mattered.

She was the one sitting in Willim Pinot's office today, not whatshisname.

Arriving at one of those two less comfortable chairs, Zina Nichols sat down and, breathing in the sheer power that permeated the area, curled her fingers around a pair of genuine leather armrests.

Exhaling, she settled in.

Yes, she thought. *I could get used to this.*

A check of her dataclip — the tiny device attached to one ear and feeding signals through her ear canal and into her brain — said it was 1645.

Patience, she thought.

The door slid open.

Chapter 2

Location: Arlington, Virginia
Local Date: June 30, 2252
Local Time: 1645

"Good afternoon, Ms. Nichols," Pinot said as he entered.

Zina craned her neck to watch him.

He was a big man in both height and girth. He wheezed as he made his way around his desk, moving at a pace that gave him the appearance of being busy. An aroma of stale coffee followed him. "I'm sorry to have kept you waiting."

"It's not a problem, sir."

The director, a man in his middle seventies, settled into the large chair behind the desk. His hair wisped over his ears, his cheeks were jowly, and the overall tone of his skin was closer to paste than peach. But his gaze was sharp, and his posture said it was time to get to business.

"I enjoy mentoring young talent," Pinot said, adjusting belly girth and sitting up. "But they're usually further along in their careers than you are. Why don't we start with you telling me something about yourself?"

"I appreciate that, Director," Zina said. "And it would be an honor to be a protégé of yours, but I'm not here to ask for mentorship. I'm here to offer my service."

Pinot's expression was a frown.

"All right," he said. "And what service might that be?"

"Storyteller."

"Storyteller?"

"Exactly."

"I'm afraid you're going to have to be more specific with your plot," Pinot said with a smile that was somewhere between amused and condescending. "Why would I be in need of a storyteller?"

Despite her nerves, she gave him a practiced smile that was mostly eyes.

"Because Oscar Pentabill is dead, and because you sent Ambassador Black to remove him."

Pinot sat back into his seat as if to find a better position from which to survey her. His fingers slowly rose to his chin, elbows resting on the chair's arm.

Zina took satisfaction from the almost imperceptible cock of Pinot's head that confirmed she had surprised him.

"That's quite the large leap you've just made."

"Maybe it is," she said. "But maybe it isn't."

Sitting precisely upright, Zina let an essence of Pinot's bemusement touch her own expression and watched as calculations flowed behind his passive glaze.

Relax, she told herself.

Control was everything now.

Control said confidence, and she was confident she was right.

Ambassador Torrance Black was one of several science ambassadors, a group of mostly academia-steeped political officers, that the UG used ostensibly to help leverage resources into the most useful projects. But it was also a role that allowed that same government to keep track of those same ambassadors. Torrance Black was a unique case. He was a public hero, having long ago played a pivotal role in thwarting Universe Three's attack on *Everguard*. But his propensity to push debunked theories about life in the Alpha Centauri system meant that much of the scientific community also considered him to be an academic quack of sorts.

He had been harmless enough, but still a figure worth tracking.

"Let's just say it's an interesting leap for a Grade E analyst to make," Pinot finally said.

"Did paygrade make a difference when you were my age?"

"Maybe it did," Pinot said. "And maybe it didn't."

"Touché."

Pinot's gaze grew colder then.

Zina's heart rate spiked, and her eyes locked with the director's.

It was time — put up or shut up.

"Grade E or not, I know how to sort things that matter from things that don't. I know how to pay attention, and I've seen enough information that, from my position, makes it not too much of a leap to say that you assigned the science ambassador the task of removing Oscar Pentabill."

"So. Just to be clear here. You *are* actually sitting in my office and accusing me of assassinating Oscar Pentabill?"

"I wouldn't call it assassination, sir."

"And what *would* you call it?"

"I'd call it ... maybe ... protecting the Solar System."

"Hmm. Tell me more."

"Politicians are assassinated," she said. "Threats are neutralized."

When the corner of one lip edged upward and he leaned forward in his seat, Zina knew she had him.

Pinot regarded her silently.

"You're interviewing for a job, aren't you?"

"That depends on whether there's a job available."

"All right, then, young storyteller," Pinot said. "Lay it out for me. Show me what things matter."

If she hadn't envisioned this conversation a hundred times in the quiet of her own headspace, the weight to his gaze would have smothered her. Instead, she let go of the armrests and knitted her fingers together.

"It matters," she started, "that you met with Torrance Black in the days before the conference." Pinot's expression revealed no shock that she had found record of that meeting, which she found comforting because that meant he was taking her seriously.

"And it matters that, later that day, Black's itinerary was adjusted to attend the conference at which Pentabill met his demise."

"Why is it problematic that a science ambassador went to a convention of top physicists?"

"Because the courier who arrived at Black's compartment at the

Jovian Science Center on Europa Station the night before his departure matters too."

She paused to ensure Pinot would keep up.

"It matters that the delivery was a triple blind op. So clean that the guy delivering what he thought was takeout that night couldn't possibly have a clue that what was in the package he dropped off would be able to kill a person outright."

"And what would it be in that package?"

"Virus-delivered bionite concentrate. Built and stored in a lab on Europa under register OC9, Lot Code 1505."

"Impressive," Pinot said.

"I know I don't really need to tell you, but I can also confirm the storage registers in that production facility no longer show one vial unaccounted for. I also know I don't need to tell you that the concentrate was a set of RNA-activated sequences that would pump a person's heart until it blew, then would dissolve into tissue without a trace."

A shift came in the room's tenor.

Pinot breathed in a raspy breath, *tsked*, and shook his head in a motion informed by sarcasm.

"Until it blew?" he said.

His tone confirmed her assumption. She had won. Willim Pinot knew the work and intuition it had taken to piece together every step she had just laid out, and so he knew she could go further.

She made a dismissive motion with one of her thin hands.

"I don't pretend to be a doctor. Would myocardial infarction, leading to heart attack sound better?"

"Much."

"No question it had to be done, though," Zina said. "Oscar Pentabill was confirmed as funneling advanced work to Universe Three, and you can't have that going on. Time was short — and I'd guess resources were even shorter. You did what you had to do."

"Which was?"

"Extort the ambassador. I wouldn't presume to guess precisely what you had on him but working backward it all adds up. Torrance Black was available, he had obvious access. He was also easy to burn if things went hot, which they clearly did — though I'm not sure exactly why yet. I'd storyboard it to say the ambassador was supposed to inject the bioweapon then get out of the picture, but something went haywire, and Pentabill went over the rail instead." She paused. "It's an unanticipated twist that Black is missing."

Pinot's gaze relaxed a notch. He scratched at thin stubble growing on his chin. "Spy work is a shitty game."

"Black was supposed to simply go back to his life — fade into the woodwork. But now the ambassador is a high-profile person who's gone missing, so there's going to be a scandal. The press doesn't have the resources they need to tie things into a real bow, but they're already questioning things no one wants questioned. If they keep rummaging around, they're likely to cause more than a bit of a disturbance."

She paused again, then continued when Pinot simply gestured her to.

"You're already working to drive the narrative. I see that, too. You're dropping parts of the story we'll need to make Black out as a co-conspirator with Pentabill. It's a good thread, too. It's got legs. I mean, it's going to take a little work, but it can be done."

"Hence your service?"

"I particularly like the bits revisiting the facts around *Everguard*. That, while history blamed the attack on *Everguard* on a Universe Three turncoat, that same turncoat just happened to be Science Ambassador Black's best friend throughout the entire fifteen-year flight. That's quite an elegant trail."

"Thank you," Pinot said.

"I'd expect the last shoe to drop soon — Black, a U3 agent, killed Pentabill because he was getting ready to go double and expose other agents."

"You *are* sharp."

She shrugged. "Terrorists eating their own is a good story. It's the right play."

"And the chapter you think you can add?"

"Thomas Kitchell's," she replied.

"I see."

Pinot sank into his chair and folded his fingers to make a steeple that he rested his chin on.

She had not flattered Pinot. The story the UGIO was concocting was good.

But people liked Torrance Black, bumbling or not. The director had to know, as Nichols did, exactly how thin the ice he was skating on was. The world wasn't likely to believe Black was double agent — at least not without some help.

Thomas Kitchell, one of Black's closest associates since as far back as the *Everguard* fiasco — the kid Torrance Black had infamously taken under his wing, who had played a heroic part of his own during the Universe Three attack, and who had gone on to make a career of his own — could provide that help.

Or not.

Zina wanted to lay on Kitchell a little. Wanted to make that help happen. She trusted Willim Pinot to put those pieces together here in his office and make the same assessments she had.

The director held a deep breath, then let it out in a shallow stream.

"All right," Pinot said. "Let's talk about that job opening."

NEWS

SOURCE: INFOWAVE — NEWS for the 23rd century
TRANSMITTED: June 22, 2252, Earth Standard
HEADLINE: Recent Skirmish Raises Questions

United Government Interstellar Command officials today released declassified data describing methods their scientists were using to triangulate the possible whereabouts of the terrorist group Universe Three's primary location.

This action comes after recent U3 strikes against populated stations on or around Venus, Mars, Uranus, and the asteroid mining belt. Reports also note that UG scientists confirmed the reception of indecipherable but cohesive radio signals from the Alpha Centauri tri-star system. They declined, however, to connect the two.

"Given the time we've been involved in these skirmishes, it would not be surprising if the renegades have split into multiple outposts," said Sector Admiral Omir Lassiter. "As such we're deploying listening telescopes and other ground-based processing personnel to keep our feelers out. There is no reason to think recent signals received from Alpha Centauri are related to any increase in U3 activity."

The UG statement was accompanied by a press kit that included technical reports and data cubes encoded with chronal frequency shift information from every science-oriented UGIS Star Drive jump over the past standard year — as well as a historical archive of signal processing algorithms analysts have been using to piece together tracking projections in the past. In hopes of increasing the fidelity of calculations, the package includes a toolkit that analysts have used to map a wide array of extrasolar radio emissions.

"We're learning more about how Star Drive propulsion systems interact with the universe as time goes by," Admiral Lassiter said. "It's likely we can find chronal images left behind when these machines work. If that turns out to be correct, and if we can find a collection of these profiles related to U3 Star Drive missions, then we will know where to look. We encourage anyone interested in helping to dig through this data to report any interesting findings per instructions included in the kit."

Critics argue that the UGIS approach is too lackadaisical, but Lassiter disagreed.

"Our approach is systematic, not lackadaisical. It places certainty

at the top of the priority chain rather than speed, but the citizens of the Solar System deserve safety and expect results. Space is very big, but there are still only so many places a renegade group as big as Universe Three can hide.

"The steady hand will prevail," Lassiter added. "We have professionals working on this, and the last thing we need to do is to expend Star Drive missions on frivolous exploration of what are probably random space noise.

"Time is on our side."

ICARUS DOWN

Chapter 3

Apogee: 37 Gem System
Local Date: C12/D10
Local Time: 1/9:15

"Don't worry after me," Katriana Martinez had said. *"I'll do whatever it takes to save my people."*

Deidra Francis rubbed fatigue from her temples as she tried not to think about those words, the last uttered by Katriana in the moments after they had said their last goodbyes.

She'd understood.

After everything that had happened in both their lives, Deidra understood the undying sense of loss and the deep edge of *anger* that could drive a person to do whatever they felt needed to be done to right a wrong. Deidra was willing to do that same thing — *whatever it takes* — to keep the people of Universe Three safe.

Still, waiting was hard.

She remembered the determined expression on Katriana's face as Deidra had left her on the bridge of *Icarus*.

Deidra was alone in her office on Apogee now, late in the morning. Wired and jittery from too much tea. Lacking sleep and feeling the stress that came from the unrelenting pressure of waiting for news she knew would come only on its own timeline.

Professor Catazara's team had already placed one end of a wormhole gate into a black hole, and the *Icarus* mission's goal was to embed the business end of that same wormhole into Alpha Centauri A — thereby feeding the star to the ravenous singularity at the other end.

It was a suicide mission but one that would also strip the fuel source from every Star Drive spaceship attached to the star — both their own and those of the United Government. The decision to sacrifice their own ability to make interstellar jumps to keep the UG from doing the same had been a difficult series of conversations, but the council had come down on the side of protection.

They were losing ground to the Uglies' production capacity.

And, while looking for Apogee may well be like trying to find a needle in a galaxy-sized haystack, a haystack — no matter the size — was finite.

It was only a matter of time before the Uglies found U3's base.

Deidra wallowed in the idea.

They had already lost too much to UG battle cruisers. Another such attack would spell the end.

Better no Star Drive jumps — even their own — than leave UG able to explore.

Hence the mission.

Which should be complete by now.

Deidra understood they would never hear from *Icarus* again, but she and the rest of her staff were waiting on other metrics.

Some noted that simply jumping their own craft would answer the question, but she felt the pragmatism of timing and coordination called for caution on that front. Without absolute certainty, U3 might time such jumps poorly. If they jumped *Defender* to another system, for example, and then the gate was set, they could strand even more people and another vital resource.

So, instead, the metric was more complex, and took more time to gather through the network of intelligence operatives they had spread throughout the Solar System.

Were the Uglies jumping?

If that was true ... if the Uglies *were* jumping ... then the mission had failed and the loss of Katriana Martinez and the rest was for naught.

That was the thought, anyway. Catazara's math said the gate should work quickly.

Her eyes felt dry now, her mind fought to focus.

A shower would be nice, she thought as she chugged more tea.

It didn't help.

A backrub would be nice, too. If there were anyone to give her one.

As was much of the governing center, Deidra Frances's personal office was open to the elements — or, better said, its walls were retractable and were now pulled open to reveal the settlement below. Opening those walls was something she made a practice of doing whenever the weather allowed, a form of commonsense communication she had inherited from her father, Casmir Francis, who had been the leader of Universe Three before the Uglies had killed him.

Open doors say trust, her father had said. *And trust is stronger than position.*

Deidra had grown to accept his truths even if sometimes those truths made progress difficult. She would never be as good at navigating conflicts as he had been. She was sometimes still too quick to react, and sometimes quick to anger. So, showing herself to the public could, on occasion, cause problems. But in the end, she had to agree her father had been right.

It was good to show the people doing the hardest of the work that their leadership was accessible. Things like open walls helped people see her heart was in the right place, and that mattered.

Besides, she liked how it felt when the walls were retracted.

She'd been thinking of her father often the past few days, but his aura was particularly strong this morning.

He would be proud of her.

At least she hoped he would be.

Under her leadership this Universe Three colony had first come to Apogee. And they had been here for long enough now to think of themselves as fully established.

After a long and hard struggle, the colony's agriculture was beginning to yield steady results, and sturdy shelter for the entire population was nearing completion. Life was still a battle, but resources were plentiful, and things were getting better — and so expanding the colony had become a main concern of the staff.

She stretched, pressing her feet to the floor and leaning into the stiff back of her chair.

A light breeze through the office brought earthy aromas of baking bread and early spring growth.

Plantains, she thought. The aroma reminded her of plantains.

Deidra looked to her comm system for an update that still refused to come, then gazed out to where the dome of blue sky grew purple at its edges. Though she couldn't see it this time of day, the U3 Star Drive spacecraft *Vengeance* — the command Katriana Martinez had resigned to lead the *Icarus* mission — was in orbit over that horizon.

Rocky ledges covered with green foliage rose to that bowl of blue-purple sky. Dark birds similar to hawks glided above the treetops searching for food.

The clattering of tools came from below. Muted voices called out. The damped chuffing of Thunderhoofs, brought here from Atropos, came to her as they pulled material into the lots of land the community had allocated for building. The soft whine of hover carts, too, as they moved material from one building site to the next.

The moment lifted her spirits.

She stood and went close to the rail built to protect from a fall.

Her office was on the fourth floor, high enough that she couldn't make out specific words but close enough she could hear the tones of voices, which were low and muted enough to avoid being distractions but steady enough to keep her grounded.

Kazima Yamada, Universe Three's chief engineer, and the rest of her design team had presented this location as the prime choice specifically because of its water and fertile land, but Deidra had approved it for the same reason she had approved the construction plans for the governing center — she liked the way it made her feel.

It's all for a purpose, she thought as she returned to her desk.

She had been studying another set of plans Yamada had sent her earlier this morning. She needed to get through them before this afternoon's briefing.

The door to her office opened.

A woman stood in the doorway.

"We have a report, Director."

A sudden weight came to the pit of her stomach. "And?"

"*Orion* has jumped to Galicia."

Deidra sat unmoving.

Orion. The United Government's flagship Star Drive. If *Orion* was still jumping, the wormhole gate embedded in Alpha Centauri A was still operational.

"Icarus?" she asked.

"No word."

"I see," Deidra replied. "Thank you."

The woman left and the door whisked softly shut behind.

Deidra sat back.

That *no word* combined with *Orion*'s jump meant something had gone wrong.

The black hole gate had not been engaged.

She closed her eyes, and for an instant let images flash behind her lids. Hours spent as a young girl listening to Katriana Martinez explain both the science and the art of navigation — listening as Katriana tried to explain what it felt like to become one with her spacecraft. She recalled a night sitting on a dark riverbed, drinking wine together, and talking about her lovers Kel Melody and Jamal.

A photocube of Katriana and her two girls, Rosa and Talia, came to her thoughts.

Kel Melody and Jamal, too, both lost in the United Government surprise raid that had been the first domino that convinced them all that the sacrifice of *Icarus* was one they had to make.

Gone.

All of them were gone now.

As was her father.

As was Perigee — Ellyn Parker — a woman Deidra had never met, but who was at the heart of Deidra's core. A person's lifework is built on its connections to other lives, and Deidra's traced a direct line to Ellyn Parker.

As were countless others.

But the strongest memory of all of them was still that of Kel Melody.

Deidra could still recall how she smelled. The way she traced her fingertips over Deidra's forehead and cheekbones, drawing with the lightest touch down her jawline to finish at her lips.

The sound of voices from below broke through the grayness of her thoughts.

People working in the village area.

Hammer blows falling.

The raw grate of saw on wood.

Feeling invisible weight settle over her, Deidra glanced back to the documents on her desk, then took in as much air as her lungs would allow.

The agenda to this afternoon's staff session was supposed to be about her leadership group coming to consensus on the future direction of the colony's expansion, but this news meant that agenda would have to change.

Giving a final sigh, she toggled her intercom system.

"Yes, Director?" came the reply.

"Please let the staff know I still want a session this afternoon. Ask them to check their comm queue and come prepared."

"I will."

"Thank you," Deidra said. She picked up her datapad and began to form her arguments, already feeling momentum gaining behind her.

There would be time to mourn properly later.

She had work to do now.

Chapter 4

Apogee: 37 Gem System
Local Date: C12/D10
Local Time: 2/1:00

A pall hung over the group as Universe Three's leadership gathered in the central meeting area, their mood dark and infused with something that may have been battle fatigue or might simply have been grief born of lost opportunity.

The loss of *Icarus* had been expected, but the failure of the mission brought on a sense of desperation none of them had been willing to face until now.

They had been so close.

So near to being able to live in a world where the ominous presence of the United Government could have been lifted. Now their conversations were hushed by news that they had lost *Icarus*, Captain Martinez, and her skeleton crew for nothing in return.

The muted rumble of their conversations was a steady hum in the assembly room, which was round in shape and placed at the center of the building complex. Its ceilings were tall, the room spanning two floors of the building's four. In keeping with the core aesthetic of the facility, the roof had been retracted, leaving sunlight to pour in and create a sharp, slanted shadow that scored the wall as 37 Geminorum traced its path toward the horizon.

It was late afternoon, growing toward evening.

Peak heat had receded, and the air was turning crisp.

Eyes turned toward Deidra as she entered.

"Our original agenda called for us to discuss Chief Engineer Yamada's proposal to split the settlement," Deidra said as she took her place at the table. "And we will continue to discuss those proposals when the time is better. But we've all seen the reports. We know what they mean. So now we need to come to a working consensus on how to react."

Expressions around the room said everyone understood.

Gregor Anderson cleared his throat to draw attention. His dark eyes were sunken into deep sockets, and the skin over his cheeks was loose and folded down into jowls. His bony knuckles clutched the head of a carved walking stick that let him maneuver when he wasn't on the hover chair he used for his basic transportation. He was the first to reply, his voice old and gruff.

"Before we come to any conclusions, we should jump *Vengeance* or *Defender* to Alpha Centauri A to confirm *Icarus*'s status."

The fact that it was Gregor Anderson helped Deidra refrain from responding immediately.

Anderson had been her father's closest confidant. He had lost a son to the effort against the Uglies, so had a gravitas built of sacrifice. But he was also out-of-date now and he could sometimes be slow to come off his positions even when they were lost. He had earned the respect he was due, but he was no longer a person whose opinion was always well-crafted.

Deidra had known the elder would push for such an action, though — Anderson was conservative by demeanor, and to be fair, the idea had merit.

She glanced toward the wall where Professor Catazara sat so demurely.

His gaze was downcast, and his dark skin seemed even darker in the shaded section of the room. The sleeves of his rumpled shirt were rolled up over his elbows. Though Catazara said the physics that defined wormhole gates suggested the transfer of matter from the star to the black hole he had tied to should be rapid, he also hedged his bet by saying he wouldn't rule anything out.

Given Catazara's hedge, it was still technically *possible* that the *Icarus* mission had been a success — that the wormhole was working, but that the matter transfer from the star to the black hole could take time.

So, on its own, Gregor's proposal was not outlandish.

It would be good to know exactly what had happened to *Icarus*.

But there were counterarguments to consider, and Deidra knew those other angles would come up on their own if she didn't spout them too soon. She also knew those arguments would play better coming from someone else.

It turned out that "someone else" was Timmon Keyes, the man Deidra had assigned to command *Vengeance* after Katriana had volunteered for *Icarus*.

Keyes wore simple clothes today, dark pants and a sharply cut shirt, off-white with sleeves that came to his wrists. A trim row of buttons made of polished wood closed the cuffs. The outfit spoke to his position without being a uniform in itself. He sat at the table with the clear-eyed, rigid bearing of someone who had been commanding star jumps for years — which he had. Keyes had been involved in many of Universe Three's most dangerous raids on UG outposts.

"Timing would seem critical now," Keyes said. "Running a recognizance mission in the Alpha Centauri system might well cost us initiative."

"Initiative for what?" Anderson snapped back.

Wary to avoid disrespecting the elder, Keyes picked his reply carefully.

"I agree that a search mission to Alpha Centauri would help us understand what went wrong. But we need to consider the idea that, rather than simply failing its mission, *Icarus* could have met resistance. The mission could have been derailed through direct action from the United Government themselves. If that is the case, it only stands to reason that they anticipated our effort."

"And," Yamada jumped in, "that would mean they could know a lot more about our situation than we think. They could be lying in wait if we return. To lose another Star Drive would cripple us."

Anderson scowled.

With the loss of *Icarus*, the Universe Three fleet consisted of only two craft capable of star jump: *Defender* and *Vengeance*. Production lines would begin working to build new craft soon, but the entire staff understood they had lost their momentum, and that the United Government's capacity for building new machines would now always dwarf their own.

Keyes continued Yamada's train of thought.

"If the UG gaze is diverted toward the Alpha Centauri system, we have a moment to retaliate. If we want to seize it."

Silence ensued.

While the gathering fidgeted, Keyes and Yamada exchanged glances that made Deidra wonder how deeply their relationship had gone. The two had similar personalities, both contemplative and thorough. They had worked together before, too. If they had become a couple, they could make an imposing pair — or a dangerous one, depending.

She didn't want the session to break down into arguments yet, so she nudged the conversation.

"Those are all prudent points," Deidra said. "But there are others we might want to discuss, so I suggest we move on."

"Are you asking us if we think the UG will be able to find us now?" It was Deego Larsi, the group's logistics director.

"That's certainly one question. Or if not now, *when*. But we have discussed that before — no one thinks they'll find us *now*, so those are longer-term issues. There are things more relevant in the short term."

Larsi shrugged. "What else should we care about?"

Deidra turned to Dr. Catazara. "Jorge?"

The aging professor pressed back into his hard-backed seat, then cocked his head like he often did when asked about obscure theories. Deidra hoped he had read her summary from earlier in the day.

"You're worried about the other end of the gate," he said. "The one we've already attached to the black hole. You want to know if it is going to implode on itself."

"Yes. It's a real situation now. Not a hypothetical. We've still got an active remote connection to a black hole to think about, and it seems prudent to ask how long that connection can last without being paired up."

He shrugged. "The construct we cast into the black hole is stable."

"But for how long," Yamada said. "And what happens when it fails?"

Catazara turned to the slim woman standing beside him.

"What do you think, Allie?"

Allie Feder curled her hands into balls for a moment, then wrapped her long fingers over her biceps. She was tall and, for her late twenties, still gangly. Her face was smooth, and she wore her bronzy red hair pushed to one side. While Catazara was the genius who first developed the ideas that led to remote gate technology, Allie Feder had done the heavy lifting when it came to both the development of the equations and their implementation. The young woman was brilliant. Still, her nerves were obvious.

"The throat tensors don't show any singularities," she said.

"For us non-physicists," Deidra said, "what does that mean?"

Feder blushed. "There's no reason to think the gate will close anytime, really."

"Never?" Deidra said.

"In theory."

"And in practice?" Yamada snipped from across the room.

Ever the pragmatic engineer, Yamada had sparred with Catazara in the past, clearly finding the man as eccentric as his conceptual approach was frustrating to work with, but she had to respect his background and the reputation that comes with being right about a fundamentally world-changing theory.

Feder was another situation all together.

The two often had disagreements in which the gloves seemed to come off.

"There could be losses, I'd guess," Feder said.

"You'd guess?"

The young woman pressed her lips together. "I don't know. No one has ever *been* inside a black hole, so any instabilities there would, by definition, be hard to predict through anything but empirical methods. The math we understand says the construct should be stable, though."

"So, can we still use it?" Martin Scalese piped up for the first time.

"The black hole?" Catazara said.

"Right."

"You mean can we attempt to connect it to another gate?"

"Yes," Scalese said. "That's what I mean. Could we send another follow-on mission to complete the job?"

"And lose a second ship?" Anderson quipped, his voice gruff and gravelly.

Scalese scowled.

He had come through the ranks, starting in communications, then moving through engineering, construction, and security before Deidra asked him to lead that same communications team which — in Universe Three's organizational structure — was a tough job, half tech, half spy, requiring a deep understanding of information processing and signal transfer across interstellar space as well as being able to sense the nuances of people who operated in different worlds. The role was focused on maintaining contact not only with members here on Apogee, but also with a vast network of secret agents and underground resistance fighters in the Solar System.

Scalese had taken to it perfectly.

His jack-of-all-trades background gave him a holistic sense of intuition that he used to bring disparate bits of information together in ways that suddenly made sense. He had a natural inclination for knowing where the team would need information from and getting contacts into those places. If U3 had anything resembling a secret intelligence service, Scalese's group would be it.

As they grappled with the situation, Deidra watched her staff work.

It was a trick her father had used often — if one could call patience and confidence a trick. She was going to win. She was the director. She had been fiery when she was younger, and the staff had followed her well enough simply because she was Casmir Francis's choice. But that could only last so long. The leadership of Universe Three was solid now. Deep and experienced. They followed her today because she had proven she would listen to them. With time and a little bending of elbows, she could get her way.

But she understood that what she had to propose now was large enough that she needed to gauge the room before getting to it. Sitting silently, watching while the gathering absorbed the situation let her make assessments.

"We still need more information," Anderson said, unmoved. "We don't know what happened on *Icarus*, and as a result we don't know what the United Government is doing — or even *if* they're doing anything."

"Oh, they are doing *something*, all right," Scalese piped up.

"And what would that *something* be?" Yamada said.

"I don't know," he replied, "They're running patterns in their Star Drive flights that gives it a systemic feeling, though — they've been doing similar things for some time, but there's something bigger going on now."

"How so?" Deidra asked.

"They're still stepping through systems with habitable planets, ostensibly looking to find mineable resources, but they aren't leaving colonies behind anymore."

"No colonies?" the logistics-minded Larsi asked.

Scalese shook his head. "They've always doubled up their missions in the past, looking to leverage anything they find. But no colonies. Even if they report rich resources. No settlements. No production facilities. Nothing. So, I have to think they have to have something else in mind."

"Something like finding us," Keyes said.

Scalise spread both hands over the tabletop. "That makes more sense than any other idea we've batted around. I see no other reason UG forces would be paging through habitable systems and not taking immediate advantage of them. To make matters worse, though, they've changed the pattern."

"A new pattern?" Deidra said, quizzically. "I haven't heard anything about a new pattern."

"It's fresh information," Scalese said, sheepishly. "Whereas they were once jumping to every habitable place in a system before moving on, they've started picking only one or two locations."

"What does it mean?"

"We're working on it, but it takes time to get agents into the right places."

A new voice interrupted — agricultural director, Kyleen Lian. "I'd guess they've accelerated their search by focusing only on the most likely biological targets. That's what I would do if I were them, anyway. Focus on places that could support large settlements rather than dig deeply into every nook and cranny. It's how we make our decisions, after all, or at least it's a key factor."

Deidra took in a breath and nodded. "If they don't find us at the top one or two locations in a system, move on."

"That would make sense," Scalese replied. "Especially if they can determine that with reasonable precision before getting there."

"How much could that speed their search?" Anderson asked.

"We've always thought that it could take them years to find us with their original approach, years as in decades. But it would eventually work. Maybe this cuts it in half?"

It was an estimate no one wanted to hear, but Scalese wasn't finished.

"Reports also say they're still accelerating the rate at which they are building Space Drive craft, too. So..." He shrugged. "More spacecraft available would also serve to speed things up more."

Deidra gazed at Catazara, then Feder.

"Could they be doing anything else?"

"What do you mean?" Catazara responded, his eyes becoming hooded.

"I mean," Deidra said, "what if Gregor is right to worry? What if the Uglies *were* lying in wait for *Icarus*, and the mission was interrupted? What are the chances, then, that they've captured the ship and that their physicists can now reverse-engineer your concept of remote gate placement?"

"Reverse engineer our device?"

Deidra nodded, growing impatient with Catazara's trait of restating every question she asked. "And if they do, could they use one of the wormhole pods we developed in such a way as to find us now?"

Catazara shrugged.

Allie Feder wrung her hands.

"Reverse engineering is difficult," Catazara said. "I doubt they could track anything back to us quickly. But I could see them working out the process of setting remote gates — and that alone would change the game."

Feder added. "Science isn't proprietary, though. So, even if they don't have one of our pods, someone will find that technology sometime no matter what."

Captain Keyes cleared his throat. "It all adds up to say we need to set that black hole gate now," he said. "Maybe we can find a way to automate more aspects of the process so loss of additional spacecraft can be minimized. Or maybe Dr. Catazara's team can invent a new way to set the gate without sacrificing any more ships? I admit I don't know what I'm talking about in that area. But we need to shut down the UG Star Drives, even if that means sacrificing another spacecraft."

The idea settled on the staff, and Deidra felt the time was right.

"There's another option," she said.

The staff turned to her.

"An option that eventually removes the problem, yet leaves our own Star Drives operational."

From the corner of her eye, she saw a shadow cross Gregor Anderson's expression.

When she was sure she had full attention, Deidra spoke. "We *do* fly another mission, as Captain Keyes suggested. And, as Martin has proposed, we *do* set a new gate opposite our ravenous little black hole. But we don't fly that mission to Alpha Centauri."

An audible gasp came from Yamada.

Scalese seemed to catch onto the idea, too, but he remained silent.

Then three or four others nodded.

It was Gregor Anderson who finally voiced the full nature of the idea. "You're talking about the Solar System, aren't you?" he said, eyes grown wide. "You're talking about embedding a black hole directly into the United Government's sun?"

Deidra Francis put both elbows onto the table, then clasped her hands in front of her.

"That's right, Gregor. I'm talking about putting that black hole directly into the middle of the Solar System."

DILEMMA

Chapter 5

Lunar University: Mare Imbrium
Local Date: July 2, 2252 (Earth Standard)
Local Time: 0745

From the quiet of his hotel room, Thomas Kitchell, dressed in only his suit pants and an undershirt, gazed over the harsh lunar landscape, letting his gaze take in the immaculate line of white regolith matched against the dark space above. That line bothered him today. He felt a powerful surge, a disquieting sense of dread building at the edge of that horizon.

He had showered and shaved, though he didn't know why now.

It was Torrance, of course.

Everything he felt since the news of his old friend's disappearance had been about Torrance Black. He had recalled their first meeting a hundred times already, that time in Torrance's system command room where he first realized Torrance was sincere in his offer to help a crappy teenager find something he was good at. He remembered the times Torrance Black had visited him as he recovered from being shot. He recalled their last conversation, too. Brief and to the point about the signal he'd captured from the Alpha Centauri system. And he remembered other times, too — moments during the *Everguard* attack. The killing of Malloy. Recovery.

He didn't know what to feel about news that Torrance was

missing.

Worried. Anxious. Uncertain.

The bright blaze of Aldrin Station — where *Everguard*'s demise had come — hovered over the horizon.

He couldn't believe Torrance was gone. Couldn't comprehend a world without him in it.

But now this darkness had moved beyond shock and loss, and into the area of his personal space. People would want something from him now. Comments or speculations or remembrances. He felt that pressure build.

I just want to be left alone.

The thought came through his haze as he stared at the razor's edge outside his window.

It was true, he thought. He didn't want to be at the forefront. All he wanted was to be able to do his work. It had been true his whole life.

With the fingertips of one hand, he touched the pane of radiation-hardened glass.

It had been years since Kitchell studied at LUMI, but the precision of the moonscape brought memories back — joy rides taken in skimmers, jousting with classmates as they soared over the surface. He recalled studying the mechanics of low-gravity fall along a ridge nearby and doing entry-level geological work to prove — once again — that the moon had never played home to organic life.

A lot had occurred since those days.

He'd made a good career for himself, good enough anyway that — as a prize-winning dignitary — the school's administration had invited him back to give a paper on the frequency signature of sub-foam beams, and big enough that news of his appearance attracted a gathering of the best technical minds in the system.

News of the events on Florecer, however, had brought the entire convention to a halt.

Oscar Pentabill was dead, and now confirmed to have been an agent of the Universe Three terrorist organization.

Torrance Black was missing — something Kitchell now felt he should have guessed last night simply because he'd waited up to talk with Torrance through ABKE about a nuance he'd found in those same Eden files they had talked about days before, the same files both of them had been studying for so long the files seemed like a part of the air they breathed.

Then came word that investigators had found Torrance's DNA in Pentabill's room — which also showed signs of a scuffle.

Rumors suddenly washed over the university like the solar wind.

So deep was his discomfort that the chirp of the hotel messenger service startled him.

The system chirped again.

"Answer," he said aloud, wondering if it might be the conference coordinator with whatever the new schedule they had devised might be.

"One moment," the system responded.

He blew a tired breath, feeling the reality of his room crashing back onto him.

He'd really been out of it.

Beside him, his toast, jam spread on one side, was still only half eaten. He picked it up, then set it back down when he realized he wasn't hungry.

A moment later the system gave a tone to say the line was connected.

"Hello. This is Thomas," he said.

"Good morning, Mr. Kitchell." A firm but feminine voice came through the system. "My name is Zina Nichols, I'm the primary investigator for the United Government Intelligence Office's inquiry into Oscar Pentabill's death. I'm wondering if you might have some time to meet with me."

"Um ... of course. What can I do for you?"

"I'd rather do this in person."

"All right. I think I've still got a talk to give today, but I can travel any time after that. When would you want to meet?"

"I don't think you understand, Mr. Kitchell. I'm in the hotel now, so I'm ready to speak as early as you're ready."

In the hotel now?

The whole conversation caught up to him.

Primary investigator?

UGIO?

He'd been thinking about press before, but given his relationship with Torrance, it made sense that investigators would want to talk to him. This felt sudden, though. What were they looking for? What did they think he knew about Oscar Pentabill?

"I'm not sure I can be of much help."

"I'm just looking for some simple background, Mr. Kitchell. Nothing to worry about."

Kitchell's dataclip said it was 0752 local. He wanted to think. "I need to clean up from breakfast."

"How's 0830, then?"

"That sounds good."

"Excellent. We'll be in the secure meeting hall on level two. You know where that is?"

"Yes, I do."

"Very good. I'll see you then."

"I'm looking forward to it."

The tone chimed to note the investigator had broken the connection.

Kitchell stared again out over the lunarscape. A chill ran down his spine.

He didn't like the feel of this.

What am I getting into?

Unfortunately, he didn't have any answers.

He took a bite of the toast. Despite the jam, the bread was dry in his mouth.

<h1>CHAPTER 6</h1>

Lunar University: Mare Imbrium
Local Date: July 2, 2252 (Earth Standard)
Local Time: 0755

The system disconnected and, for the second time in as many days, Zina Nichols found herself patiently waiting for a man to arrive.

It was fine, though.

She stood and stretched, feeling her weight distribute as the antigravity system worked to create something closer to an Earth-standard experience. It had been too long since she'd left Earth. Her muscles struggled to adjust.

The meeting room was small but functional, comfortably decorated in neutral tones of russet and beige. The floor was sound-absorbent composite designed to be soft on the feet. A chrome-plated beverage rack lined the wall on Zina's right. The opaque walling to her left had been recessed to display a view of the Lunar surface that, to be honest, she didn't much like.

She was tired, but excited, running on a bit of adrenaline despite not being able to sleep the night before. Travel did that to her sometimes. She'd taken a redeye and come to the hotel directly after touchdown. Taking the few steps to get a better view of the regolith, she considered pulling a cup of coffee from the dispensers but worried the caffeine would put her on edge.

She wanted to be calm for this conversation.

Even tired, or *especially* tired, she wanted to be in control.

Outside, the gray-white expanse of regolith expanded to the crisp black horizon in an eternal way that fit her mood.

There was a difference, she thought, between patience and waiting.

Patience was timing.

Waiting was weakness.

Patience was finding the right moment to move, while waiting meant simply being afraid to make a decision.

One of her first dojo instructors had called her a tiny lioness, which she liked so much she had a dynamic feline image laser-inked onto her left hip. She had two such images, that lioness and a lily she'd put on her forearm as a gift to herself when she took this job.

They'd been expensive, and considerably more painful than a traditional image, but so much more than worth it.

She breathed softly through her nose, feeling the lioness image move now.

So much of her life had been about waiting for idiots to reveal themselves.

She enjoyed thinking ahead of the game, though, reveled in seeing the board shift and finding the right way to adjust her mindset to new positions. She liked the way a collection of facts smelled when she put them together in ways that made sense. When she was a girl, she hated that things came so intensely to her, but now she loved it. A young person needed to think ahead to get ahead — especially if that young person was engaged in intelligence work.

Now, alone in this crappy little conference room, Zina sensed a small victory nearing.

Thomas Kitchell may well be an esteemed scientist, but his voice had betrayed anxiety. She tasted the metallic hint of blood in the defensive tone of his conversation.

Zina put her back to the view, then leaned against the wall.

There was a security agent in the hallway outside. Lou.

She felt his presence as crisply as she felt the chill of the landscape against her back.

Zina hadn't wanted the detail assigned to her but had capitulated when Pinot had demanded it, realizing then that the director wasn't reckless enough to simply set her free to work sight unseen.

Lou's real job wasn't to protect her so much as watch her.

That, too, was fine, she thought. That, too, was good.

A moment later she heard muted footsteps coming from down the hall.

She took her seat, again, and waited.

Patiently.

Chapter 7

Lunar University: Mare Imbrium
Local Date: July 2, 2252
Local Time: 0829

The hotel carpet muted the sound of Kitchell's stride as he turned a corner and made his way down the well-lit but still dark hallway, and toward a closed conference room door at the far end, the door flanked by a dark-suited goon.

Already anxious, the sight of the man made the hair over Kitchell's neck stand up.

Unlike Torrance, Thomas Kitchell had never wanted to get involved in politics at all. Or, since Torrance was never particularly inclined toward politics either, it was better to say that Kitchell had never been willing to deal with it like Torrance had. The weeks of fallout after *Everguard* had proven that he did not like the attention of the press, let alone everyone else. That was why Kitchell mostly stayed out of things. So much easier just to take a contract and do the work rather than think great thoughts about his work's uses and ramifications. History was chock-full of examples of perfectly good technology being misapplied for nefarious results, but the big picture said that advantages always outweighed whatever disasters might come with progress.

"Will it matter in twenty-five years," one of his dissertation coaches had told him when he'd been grappling with such questions a long time ago.

Which made sense at the time.

Now, though, with questions rolling through his thoughts about Oscar Pentabill's death, and where Torrance Black might be, Kitchell didn't think anything made sense anymore.

His gaze went to the line of rounded pods running along the walls at the place where they joined with the ceiling. Sensors, he knew, part of the "secure" aspect of this zone of the conference center that Nichols had noted in their call.

Kitchell had worked on parts of these technologies in the past — active jammers, resistance filters, and AI-enabled frequency analyzers that could pick out DNA-level differences in the electrical fields each human body emitted. Intriguing projects — all conceived with the conflicting cross-purposes of recording everything that UG wanted but shredding the rest.

As he approached the door, it sensed his body signature, and slid open.

Kitchell had always thought this feature was amazing, but seeing it in practice now just served to remind him that he was being tracked.

The goon stepped aside.

The primary investigator, a trim woman, dressed in a crisp blouse of dark blue, was seated behind a desk. She was young, with dark hair. Thin to the point of tininess, her delicate hands folded together into an open-fingered butterfly resting on the table before her.

The goon entered behind him, then stood along the wall as the door slid shut.

"Ms. Nichols, I presume," Kitchell said.

"Good morning, Mr. Kitchell. Thank you for coming. It's not often I get to sit with a bona fide hero of the UG."

"It's my pleasure, I'm sure. That was a long time ago."

He took his seat, noting with distraction that holoprojector buds dimpled each corner of the table.

Settling down and then looking up at the investigator, Kitchell was struck by the sense of isolation created by the cold expanse of the table between them.

The woman had seemed birdlike at first, but now radiated an aura of calmness that said she was older than she appeared. When their eyes met, her gaze sent a flash of anxiety that raced through his body to pool in the pit of his stomach. The slight constriction around her brown eyes, combined with a barely perceptible shift in the angle of her gaze, spoke of judgement.

He felt suddenly exposed like a mouse in the open.

The air flow was gentle, though. The environment felt warm.

The juxtaposition of sensations did nothing to ease his discomfort.

The primary investigator placed a datapad on the table before her, but didn't turn it on, meaning it was more for show than function.

"Tell me about Ambassador Black," Zina Nichols said.

Though it shouldn't have, the direct nature of the question caught Kitchell by surprise.

He glanced at the datapad, then up to Nichols.

Slick presentation or not, he realized she was a low-ranking member of the UGIO, but also understood she had real power here. This combination — low-ranking, but with power to flex — made her one of the most dangerous kinds of UGIO official there was.

"Is Torrance a suspect?"

"Shouldn't he be?"

He cleared his throat.

"I've known LC for a long time, Ms. Nichols. He's a good person. What do you want to know?"

"LC?"

"His rank when I first met him. Lieutenant Commander. Everyone called him LC."

"Back when you were a teenager aboard *Everguard*, right?"

"Yeah. A long time ago. The ambassador brought me onto his team even before he saved all those lives."

Kitchell was happy with himself for adding the hero twist to his answer, but if the supportive nature of the comment caught Nichols in any way, she didn't show it.

"Can you give us any idea why Ambassador Black might have been in Oscar Pentabill's room the evening of Pentabill's death?"

"They were probably just catching up."

"Catching up?"

He shrugged.

"They'd known each other for a long time. I don't see why he wouldn't touch base."

"How would you describe their relationship?"

"Professional?"

"Is that a question?"

Kitchell scratched his chin. "I don't know what else you'd call it. I mean. They were collegial enough as far as I know. Not really friends, but they both ran in the same circles — which were … professional."

"How often did they converse?"

"I have no idea."

"Did Black have any issues with Oscar Pentabill?"

"What do you mean, issues?"

The investigator's silence and the gentle tightening of skin around her eyes told Kitchell she was the one asking questions.

Kitchell cleared his throat.

"I'm sorry," he said.

"Oscar Pentabill is dead," Nichols replied, "and Ambassador Black was likely the last person to see him alive. So let me ask again, did 'LC' have any issues with Oscar Pentabill?"

"No," Kitchell replied. "Torrance didn't have any argument with Oscar that I'm aware of."

"That you're aware of?"

"Well, I'm not that close with Torrance anymore. We mostly go our own ways. But I can't think of any issue Ambassador Black would have with Oscar Pentabill."

Nichols seemed intrigued with the response.

"No past conflicts? No unusual associations?"

"I don't know what you're trying to get at."

"I'm trying to determine what relationship existed between two men before one was killed and the other went missing."

"Are suggesting Torrance Black killed Oscar?"

"Are *you* suggesting that?"

Kitchell drew back and put his lips together. This wasn't where he wanted to go, but no quick answer popped into his head. Dampness came to his palms, and he felt heat in his cheeks. The goon behind him seemed closer than before.

"Torrance isn't a killer, Investigator. I'll put my entire reputation down on that much. I'm sure the ambassador had nothing to do with Oscar's death."

Her smile was thin-lipped. Showing no teeth.

The investigator liked her job, Kitchell realized. She laced her fingers together and put them on the table before her, leaning imperceptibly forward.

"All right," she said. "Then let's move on to your conversation with Ambassador Black before he went to the conference."

Kitchell's stomach tightened.

"What are you after?"

"You did have a conversation with Ambassador Black shortly before his trip, is that correct?"

"Yes."

"What did you talk about?"

The conversation had consisted of him giving Torrance news about an old data file that held the first messages from Eden — the planet in the Alpha Centauri system LC had once sent an "errant" wormhole pod toward in hopes that any intelligent life there could reverse-engineer their way out of whatever problem a wormhole in their home star might cause them.

Nobody but Torrance and Kitchell believed there could be intelligence on Eden, though.

Only them and the few thousand kooks who would spring up every now and again to make things worse, anyway.

The new learning he'd discovered could change that.

Pulling new data out of the signal had required intense processing, but those data had, most definitely, shown patterns that repeated in ways that strongly suggested an intelligence behind them. Polishing that data was the next chain in his process, but in as little as a couple weeks Kitchell might have something worth peer reviewing.

That's what he'd talked to Torrance about.

But Torrance had paid horribly for being too public with his ideas of intelligent life on Eden in the past — he'd been belittled, passed over for promotion, and shoved into his benign little corner as science ambassador. They both understood the pressure that would fall on them if they so much as tried to publish another "Life on Eden" piece before it was ready.

It was why he and Torrance had both decided to wait to release their findings until they were beyond sure of their stability.

Silence hung like a dagger between Kitchell and the investigator as Kitchell glanced to the window where, outside, the horizon remained a crisp black-and-white line drawn in space.

He didn't want to tell a UGIO investigator — or anyone else, for that matter — anything about the message, but the expression on Nichols's face told Kitchell there was more at stake now than simple professional reputation. He hadn't felt this kind of survival instinct since the day Universe Three had attacked *Everguard.*

"We didn't talk about anything special," Kitchell said. "I'm planning to be around JSC in a few weeks. His office on Europa Station. I wanted to see when we could get together again."

"That's not how the transcript of the conversation reads."

"If you know what we said, why ask the question?"

"This will go better if you stay with the truth."

Kitchell swallowed hard, feeling the distinct shift in the current of the conversation.

"I told Torrance that I'd found evidence of life in the Alpha Centauri system. Since you already know so much about us, you know this is a passion the two of us have shared for our entire relationship. It was only natural that I would call him directly."

"I see," Nichols replied.

She tapped a lacquered fingernail three times on the surface of her closed datapad, then leveled her gaze.

"And when did you first realize Ambassador Black had sympathies toward Universe Three?"

"What?"

"Or was that *also* a passion the two of you shared?"

A bolt of absolute confusion stifled him.

"That's absurd."

Nichols knitted her hands together.

"When did you first realize Ambassador Black had sympathies toward the terrorists?"

Seconds passed.

"Perhaps we can work together on this, Thomas," the investigator said in a calm voice. "We knew Pentabill was an agent of Universe Three well before he went to Florecer. Now we are coming to understand Ambassador Black was also associated with that terrorist organization. What I want to know is when you first understood that to be true."

Kitchell sat stunned.

A ball of anger welled in his gut.

"I'm done with this," he said, pushing his chair back and standing tall. "Torrance Black is a hero, and you know it."

He stepped toward the doorway.

The last things he remembered were the goon pressing a fingertip to his neck, and the world going gray.

Chapter 8

Lunar University: Mare Imbrium
Local Date: July 2, 2252
Local Time: 0845

Zina had barely gotten out of her chair when the security detail took it upon himself to "give Kitchell the finger," as the security community called his maneuver.

By the time her subject hit the floor, she was standing upright, mouth gaping open in what would have been a request for Kitchell to come back. Instead, she stepped around the table to see the scientist crumpled on the conference room floor.

Crap.

"Why'd you have to do that?" she asked.

"My orders were to keep him from leaving."

She scowled.

Lou was technically correct, and if he reported an angry outburst from her to Pinot it would just add to the problem, so taking Lou down a notch here was out of the question.

She used a booted toe to nudge Kitchell's leg.

He was out cold.

She could have him pumped full of something to bring him back up. That would wake him more quickly, but then he'd be hyped up and unreliable at best and at worst incapable of consistently rational thought.

If things went crazy, well.

Zina sighed.

She didn't want to create a situation where she needed to have the man killed just to cover her tracks — not for someone like Kitchell, anyway.

Still, she needed him to make a deal.

Everything added up to say she'd just have to wait until he slept off the tranquilizer.

Resigned, she turned to the guard.

"You know the drill."

"Get him to the tank?"

"Yeah. Let me know when he's up."

Chapter 9

Location: Unknown
Local Date: Unknown
Local Time: Unknown

Thomas Kitchell's thoughts swam in a gray murk.

Blurred sounds floated somewhere in the distance. His head pounded. His muscles felt stretched and cold like his body had been laid on a sheet of ice, the chill of its solid surface burning into his arms, chest, and legs.

And his cheekbone.

An icepick was pressing firmly into his cheekbone.

Yes, an icepick.

Into his cheekbone.

Jesus, his cheekbone!

Kitchell gave a loud grunt and sucked in a huge breath as he opened his eyes.

A slate-gray plane of hazy concrete splayed its woozy way toward a slanted wall and a blurred cell door. Noises came, wavy and incomprehensible.

His tongue stuck against the roof of his mouth.

Coughing in the dry air, Kitchell propped himself on his elbows. A fresh pulse of pain followed the blood flowing back to his cheekbone — a warmer pain than before, the throbbing burn of hot coal rather than the stiletto-sharp stab of floor on flesh.

Ahhhh.

His moan reverberated in the closed space.

The cell was cramped and windowless, three meters to a side. Grainy light came from luminescence in the ceiling, revealing a hardbacked chair and a ramshackle cot that reminded him of a camping trip he'd taken Earthside with friends a long time ago. The door — a tight mesh of metal bars — was a brighter white than the walls, which were bare.

Sounds beyond the gate coalesced into a combination of voices and machinery.

A clank came from somewhere outside the cell. Muted voices laughed.

Events flashed back.

The room. The investigator. The questions. Torrance Black. *Universe Three.*

The investigator hadn't been happy with his answers, and even less excited with his attempt to leave the briefing room.

Nichols, Kitchell recalled. The investigator's name had been Zina Nichols.

Ignoring the ache in his muscles, Kitchell stood, balancing himself carefully as he made a wobbly path to sit on the edge of the cot.

He was still wearing his own clothes. Still the suitcoat and pants he'd donned in his hotel room what now seemed like weeks ago.

His body felt wrung out.

He drew a cleansing breath, and, still clearing cobwebs, coughed again.

Suddenly he was hungry.

What the hell was he doing here? How long had he been here? And where exactly was *here*? He pressed his fingers over his temples, suddenly sensing the claustrophobic closeness of the walls. Someplace in the bowels of the Lunar penal system, he'd guess, but they could have jumped him anywhere.

A memory of the business end of the investigator's gaze brought him up short.

This was no game. He could be anywhere in the civilized galaxy or, depending on exactly how serious the UG was about him, any one of hundreds of other places *less* than civilized.

Cold anger grew in his gut.

Kitchell had never considered the idea that his own government would see him as a threat.

He'd worked for them, after all.

The only political arguments he'd gotten into were the kind of academic spats of hand-wringing that came from being on the leading edge of technology development, and the intellectual shit-slinging that came with supporting Torrance Black's notions regarding life in the Alpha Centauri system. He'd always considered himself a friend of the UG structure. Certainly not someone to lock away.

He'd heard talk, though — stories, rumors, and anecdotes about overbearing government officers in the chain of command getting off-kilter, and government agencies cracking down. He'd had enough close brushes with policy makers to know better than to discount that kind of story out of hand. It was certainly possible that the UGIO — of which the investigator had been part of — could make people disappear, but he'd always considered these stories to be at least a little overblown. Until now they'd always seemed more entertainment than real, more wish fulfillment than actual threat.

Now, though, things seemed different.

What was the UG doing? How long *could* they keep him here before someone noticed?

Was it possible for the UGIO to simply "disappear" a world-class scientist?

Someone would miss him, right?

He ran his hand over his scalp, feeling his temples throb as he considered the list of exactly who those somebodies might be.

Who *would* miss him?

There were his compatriots — working-level scientists all over the system, but they wouldn't matter in a real power game.

Dean Mikkula had invited him to LUMI. He had power, but not enough for this kind of situation. Mikkula had always been a win-at-all-costs kind of a player, too. Probably wouldn't play a game he couldn't beat. So, he was out.

There was Quay Ti-Taan.

As a team director at the UG Sensor Command, Ti-Taan had coordinated Kitchell's work with radiation transformation and information control. She knew exactly how essential that work had been in learning how to stitch together frayed signals that came from U3 Star Drive jumps. She could vouch that it was Kitchell's work that led to the algorithms that were in use combating the rebels today.

Ti-Taan had power, too, the right kind.

She was, however, next in line for promotion. If the UGIO was trying to take Torrance down, Kitchell didn't think the director would risk spending capital to save him.

Marisa, he thought, feeling his confidence rising a notch with her name.

Marisa Harthing had been on *Everguard*, too.

She was Torrance's life partner, and, while not formally married, the two had lived their lives in close orbit with each other, orbits that included adopting a pair of daughters together.

Marisa had been a *de facto* mother to Kitchell — an aunt, at least. The two of them had shared brief messages when news of Torrance's disappearance first circulated.

She would care.

It would take time, but eventually she would realize that Kitchell was gone. Marisa was a player in the United Government Interstellar Command, too. Which would help. She'd spent much of her career in various roles navigating Star Drive craft.

She could get him out of whatever trouble this was.

Feeling resolve, Kitchell went to the cell door.

The hallway outside ran endlessly onward to his right, but to his left the corridor opened into a larger holding room of some kind.

He was feeling a little more human now at least.

"Hey," he called, wrapping both hands around the bars and pressing against the gate. "I want to talk to someone!"

A metallic drone about the size of a football motored soundlessly down the hall, levitating with what Kitchell saw was a superconducting gravity drive. It stopped before his cell door. A ring of lights flickered at the rim encircling the machine.

"Abke," Kitchell said, assuming the drone connected to the Autonomic Bioprocessing Knowledge Engine that connected the whole of civilization as defined by the United Government. "Please inform UGIS Officer Marisa Harthing that I need to speak with her."

The rim of lights flashed blue, then green.

The cell door's locking mechanism clanked, then came a soft

buzz.

Kitchell pulled his hands back as the gate recessed into the wall with a *thunk* that reverberated down the long hallway.

"Follow," a warm voice came from the drone.

Kitchell hesitated.

What were his alternatives?

Rubbing a hand over his sore neck, he stepped into the hallway.

In the direction the machine had come from, the corridor opened into a larger room that looked like a cross between a warehouse and a locker room for the collection of robotics that were stored in rows on shelves. A bank of wide windows opened to show him a space where human controllers worked.

"Follow," the drone repeated as it moved down the opposite, longer hallway.

The idea of kicking the drone and running down the hall crossed his mind. There had to be a way out. But a glance to the controller's window told him that ignoring the drone's direction would result in force of some kind.

Despite himself, Kitchell laughed then.

He'd had enough of forced unconsciousness for one day.

"Could you at least see if I could get some food," Kitchell said as he began to follow the machine. "I think I missed lunch."

CHAPTER 10

Location: Unknown
Local Date: Unknown
Local Time: Unknown

The first stage of the corridor was as long and as spare as Kitchell might have imagined a prison's corridor to be — if he had ever tried to imagine such a thing, anyway. It was something that had never crossed his mind before, but he figured would never leave him now.

The path was wider than it was tall, with rounded walls that made it feel claustrophobic. Like walking through a cave or a pipeline.

A luminescent rail ran down the ceiling's centerline. Low, but incessant sound filled the tunnel: the clatter of metallic clanking of assembly rooms and of voices that emanated from cells that branched off from either side where inmates — or "prisoners," or whatever Kitchell himself was — were busy living whatever lives they lived.

The air was cool against his skin as he walked, but it smelled of body heat turned rancid by certain *laissez-faire* attitudes toward hygiene.

The farther he walked, the more real everything seemed to get.

There were consequences here. Lives being lived to no end.

Kitchell thought more deeply about what the investigator had said about Torrance.

It wasn't true. Torrance Black was not an agent of Universe Three. It *couldn't* be true. Could it? And yet, Torrance was gone, and the ideas behind that simple fact made Kitchell feel like the corridor was closing in on him.

What the hell was happening?

What if *nobody* could help him?

He came to another section of the compound, this one warmer and carrying the faint aroma of disinfectant. The walls appeared to be freshly painted here, too. The only sound was the intimately cloistered thuds of his own footsteps.

Finally, the drone stopped before a metallic door embossed with the number C-73.

Behind that door, to Kitchell's complete lack of surprise, was Investigator Nichols, seated at a small table of polished steel that rose from a spike at the room's center.

She wore a red blouse now rather than the blue from before — but just as crisply creased as the earlier one. Her gaze was still as sharp, too, even more so than before. The datapad of hers was there again, sitting notably at the edge of the table beside her.

The walls were green this time. Dark. Their flatness after the rounded tunnel walls made them feel deep somehow. The floors were made of the same composite tile that lined the hallway. The lighting was warmer in the interrogation room than in the hallway, or his cell for that matter — its steady illumination coming from entire span of the ceiling to filter over her and the steel table. There was more gold and orange to the spectrum here than elsewhere, though, making Kitchell understand his cell's illumination was shifted blue, presumably to give the environment a sharper edge.

"Hello again, Mr. Kitchell," Investigator Nichols said as he entered the room.

The door gave a solid sound as it shut behind him.

The chamber was large enough to hold four people comfortably, but today there were only Nichols and him

"We're alone this time," Kitchell said, absently rubbing his neck where the guard had injected him.

"Alone enough," Nichols replied, smiling in a way he couldn't interpret as she motioned the chair across from her. "Please, have a seat."

A ring of ceiling-mounted sensor pods confirmed they were

being monitored.

"No guard is a good guard, I always say," he replied, sitting. The chair was comfortably padded. "I expected something more austere."

"A dungeon could be arranged if you'd prefer."

"That won't be necessary."

The brows over Nichols's eye rose in mock relief. "That sounds promising."

"I think I see what you're doing," Kitchell said, trying to gain control. "I just don't understand why."

"Tell me more," she replied.

"It's clear you're going to destroy Torrance by attaching him to Universe Three."

"And you think that's not true?"

"Please, Ms. Nichols. It's just you and me here — you and me and whoever is behind those monitors, anyway. You've got all the power. But we both know that Torrance Black is not, and will never be, an agent for Universe Three. I would appreciate if you would not condescend as far as to ask me to pretend otherwise."

"All right, then. What do you think we're doing?"

Kitchell clasped his hands and pressed them against the table's edge, using the pressure to help focus his thoughts.

"You need me. I know Torrance Black better than anyone other than Marisa Harthing. The public knows that. If you're taking him down, people will come to me to understand who he is."

"And?"

"You want to cut a deal."

"You're a smart man," she said.

"And the deal?"

"Play this game and we'll keep Officer Harthing out of this."

Something in her tone made Kitchell's heart pound.

He hadn't thought about it from that angle, yet, but obviously the same situation happening to him would happen to Marisa, too. Or could, anyway. The investigation might spare Torrance's daughters, too, because how much of an insight do children, even adult children, really have on their parents. But Marisa Harthing had intimate history with Torrance. Kitchell imagined the investigator escorting Marisa into a room like this.

Unless...

Maybe.

A presence built around him. A net, slowly closing.

He sat back then, examining the depths in the investigator's eyes.

"You don't want to take Marisa down," he said. "You expect she'll publicly denounce the idea that Torrance was a U3 agent, but if I play the game, then you can set us against one another."

One corner of Nichols's lips twitched upward, but the rest of her expression remained impassive, giving him time to finish his own conclusions.

"And if I don't?"

Nichols leaned forward, thin forearms resting on the steel edge of the table.

"Torrance Black was a traitor, but neither you nor Officer Harthing have to be. Play ball and we won't take you with him, otherwise we'll try all three of you for treason against the United Government."

"I see," Kitchell said.

And he did.

For the first time in his life, he could see the entirety of a United Government plan laid out before him, his part and the rest, and for the first time he realized he was going to have to make a decision: Protect Torrance or save both himself and Marisa.

Torrance was already gone, and the hard expression on the investigator's face said that the chances he would ever be found were less than slim.

The idea sent a chill up his spine and over his back.

"It's up to you, Mr. Kitchell," the investigator said, pausing to cock her head in a subtle, birdlike tick. "Which would you have me do?"

NEWS

SOURCE: INFOWAVE — NEWS for the 23rd century
TRANSMITTED: July 2, 2252, Earth Standard
HEADLINE: Black Considered "Official Person of Interest" in Scientist Killing

Evan Abade, a spokesperson for the investigation into the death of leading scientist Emil "Oscar" Pentabill, confirmed today that the case is now being pursued as a homicide and has described United Government Science Ambassador Torrance Black as an official person of interest.

"Obviously, we can't get into specifics of the case," the spokesperson said. "But I can say that we have physical evidence that puts Black in the deceased's hotel room prior to the event, and it's part of the public record that the two were collaborators at several points in the past."

Witnesses have also reported that Ambassador Black left an elevator under the escort of another person shortly after Pentabill's fall occurred.

The spokesperson declined to confirm that the investigation is treating Black — who has been considered a hero for his exploits during the infamous Everguard attack — as if he were actually an agent for Universe Three. Given confirmation that Pentabill had been funneling information to U3 for decades, however, the association is not hard to consider.

If true, it would be security news of staggering proportions, leaving questions of what access he could have supplied the terrorists.

Abade concluded the statement with another request that anyone with information about Ambassador Black's whereabouts contact the investigation team as soon as possible.

"We're following every lead we have."

SOURCE: INFOWAVE — NEWS for the 23rd century
TRANSMITTED: July 3, Earth Standard
HEADLINE: Renegade Black Confirmed as U3 Agent

United Government officials today revealed that Torrance Black, who has served in various official capacities inside the United Government Interstellar Command, is now known to have been an agent for Universe Three, the terrorist group responsible for a long string of aggressive attacks on UG positions.

"It is with deep pain that I stand before you to report this news," Admiral Naomi Umaro, the top officer at Interstellar Command, said. "Torrance Black was considered a hero of the system at the time of the Everguard incident, but as a result of intense investigation it has been confirmed that he was likely working with the U3 organization even back then."

The statement goes on to suggest that U3 used the Everguard operation to cement Black's position in United Government circles, and then left him silent while he made his way through the system — touching base with him as needed via their connections with fellow scientist and U3 spy Emil Pentabill, recently murdered as a result of counterespionage.

Black remains at large and is now a clear suspect in that murder.

Authorities suspect U3 had assigned Black to assassinate Pentabill when they learned Pentabill was going to turn once again and provide UG intelligence officers with names of agents he'd worked with.

Umaro said that the United Government has officially stripped Black's rank and position, and that he is now being pursued as an enemy of the system.

STAR LINK

Chapter 11

Defender Control Room
Apogee: 37 Gem System
Local Date: C12/D13
Local Time: 2/4:17

"Program loaded in Gamma pod," the technician called from the floor of the recessed bay, pulling his gaze up from the test bird's side panel to take in the pod launch tube that loomed ahead of it.

The little craft, its gray-blue paint scrubbed away and fading, had been originally designed to be used like a wave board to "surf" a planet's atmosphere, hence served as a bit of daredevil entertainment. This one was barely spaceworthy anymore, however. Like the Alpha and Beta pods they had already loaded, it was ready for the scrap heap anyway.

Allie Feder stood on the gunmetal platform that looked out over *Defender*'s launch control room and looked at the data flow running over the panels before her.

She nodded.

"Load confirmed," she said, then rubbed her biceps with her hands — half to drive her anxiety away and half to ease the chill that permeated the open expanse of the pod bay. The place was utilitarian in its construction — a tangled network of painted girders and metallic framework. Humidity-controlled, too, which brought a sharpness to the room that she could sometimes feel beyond what she considered reasonable.

This was no bridge strategy room.

It was stark and spare, built for a purpose, no unnecessary equipment allowed.

Everything *should* work, she thought, but even she had been around long enough to know the power of that word *should.*

She also knew more than just her career was on the line here.

The idea had come in a flash as she'd been eating a pecan and raisin dessert — or at least that's what the residents of Apogee called them. Close enough, she'd thought. All she cared about was that they were delicious, that she often craved them, and that a bowl of them could take her mind off the rest of the world for a precious few spare moments. She could still recall the instant the idea came — evening time after the director's staff meeting, standing on a common patio space outside her tiny room she called "the hut." Captain Keyes had made a throwaway comment about setting a gate without sacrificing a ship, and there, on that tiny patio four hours later, lightning struck.

Allie and Professor Catazara had long ago worked out process parameters that let them cast a wormhole gate remotely, something they had used to build that first connection to the black hole to begin with. But the process had no precision. Now that they'd connected to the black hole, casting the next wormhole gate was no small risk.

Like most ideas, the concept Allie flashed on was simple at its core: launch three linked pods to triangulate a target, hence dramatically reduce the casting math.

The memory of that moment gave her a deep sense of satisfaction that emerged as a comfortable, if not whimsical smile even now.

Now they were evaluating the concept.

If the process was successful, it could change everything.

If it was successful, the mission to set the black hole pod wouldn't require the sacrifice of another ship. If her theory held water, it would save the lives of Universe Three personnel — like these techs who were working on this exercise, and who would otherwise volunteer for the mission if it meant the end of the United Government.

Loss had been hard for these people.

Something that, especially now that the first massive UG attack on Atropos had left her untethered, she understood. In its earliest days fervor in the community of Universe Three had risen on pure philosophy, but now everyone had lost someone to United Government oppression.

If Deidra Francis asked them to sacrifice their lives for the community, they would do it.

Intellectually, Allie had understood this fact even as she was devising the approach, but she hadn't truly felt the impact of the idea until she'd briefed Director Francis and saw the expression on the woman's face as comprehension grew.

Watching the technician work and seeing his gaze flash to the launch tube, she felt that same pressure.

It was a Very Big Deal, this test of hers.

"Initiate Gamma pod," she said.

The tech closed the side panel and began the process that loaded the pod into its tube.

She watched as the pod bay loaded, then the final pod tube cap swung shut with a metallic clank that reverberated off the bay's high walls.

"Pod tubes loaded," the tech called.

Allie turned to the head controller.

"Initiate the program," she said.

"Confirmed," the controller replied, then toggled in the proper launch sequences.

She paced the small platform, waiting for the telltale thumps that would announce the launches.

The terse exchanges required for efficiency's sake made her feel self-conscious. They were a little too military for her tastes, a little too formal. But she understood protocol and she understood necessity. *Defender*'s crew was experienced — familiar with the sensations that came with making dangerous runs into territories where mistakes could cost lives. They trained to follow commands and followed commands to train.

Her footsteps clanked against the metallic floor of the platform. Her mind looped over the algorithms she'd built into the tiny dimension drillers each of the test pods carried.

Would the math hold?

It was those three points in space that the casting algorithm would anchor on.

She flexed her fingers into a fist, then relaxed them.

So much could go wrong. The dimension drills — which were fragile by nature — could even be destroyed by the simple forces of launch.

"Five seconds," the head controller reported.

She ran a hand through the longest shank of her hair.

"Four."

A breath came.

"Three."

She held it. Fists clenched. Skin tingling.

"Two … one."

The launch tube reverberated.

"Linked pods away," the head controller reported. A moment later he added: "Three solid signals present. Launch is successful."

Allie exhaled, feeling relief all the way to her toes. The linked pods still had a flightpath to run, then the process of triggering the prototype gate would bring on another wave of anxiety.

One problem at a time, though.

The launch was complete, and the drillers were intact. Her work here was finished. Time to go to the bridge and wait for the results.

She checked the system clock. Ten minutes.

Tension was already rising again.

"Thank you for your work," she said to the crew.

Then Allie Feder left engineering, still feeling anxious, and began the short walk to the lift tube.

The door to the bridge slid back and Allie stepped into the room. The physical movement of traveling through the ship had helped calm her, but only a bit. Her gaze couldn't help but go to the dark expanse outside the viewport that was now open toward deep space.

She couldn't make a visual on the pods, but felt their presence, nonetheless.

"Congratulations on a successful launch," Captain Henri Shudar said.

"We're not done yet," Allie said too tersely. She took the padded seat she'd also filled when *Defender* had first launched and examined the holoprojection in the center of the room as it tracked the position of each test pod.

Shudar smiled and came to sit beside her. "What are you going to do next?" he said.

Allie smiled.

The captain was older than her by at least a local decade, but he had a way about him that made Allie feel comfortable. Moreso than Captain Keyes, anyway. Both Shudar and Keyes were well regarded, having both been part of the earliest insurgency against the Uglies, and having both commanded multiple forays into UG territory. But while Allie had always felt quite comfortable to be around Henri Shudar, something about Keyes set Allie on edge. It was why Allie had asked to use *Defender* for the prototype run. She had enough to worry about without trying to deal with the ship's captain.

Now Shudar was trying to take Allie's mind off the problem.

"I'm sorry, Captain. I didn't mean to snap."

"It's all right," Shudar replied.

"No, it's not."

"You need to get used to the pressure, I think," the captain replied. "You're very good at what you do, so you're only going to be able to hide behind the professor for so long."

"That's supposed to make me feel better?"

"Yes," the captain enunciated in a firm but warm voice. "It is."

Allie chewed the corner of one lip, then ran her hand through her hair again. It was a nervous tick, she knew, one that annoyed her every time she did it.

"There are three pods out there because of you, Allie Feder," Shudar said. "Maybe they will work, and maybe they won't. But I've seen your efforts for a while now. I'd be willing to bet your insides already know what is going to happen. You're just not willing to trust them yet."

Allie nearly laughed. "You have no idea."

"Sure, I do."

Shudar turned his gaze toward deep space then, and Allie felt a sense of calm around the captain that seemed to bleed right into Allie herself. She opened her mouth to ask a question that she didn't know was coming when the science station interrupted.

"Triangle set."

The three markers for the pods sat at their programmed places in the holoprojection.

It was time to trigger the dimensional drills.

Allie stood, suddenly feeling every inch of her body tingle.

The captain smiled up at her, the expression both serene and encouraging.

Captain Shudar had been right. Now that the physical transport of the drills was finished, Allie knew the system was going to work.

"Engage the drills," she said.

A minute later the guideposts had been set. Three holes pierced the quantum foam. They were small rents, only molecules wide, but they were enough.

The remote gate system was a success.

Chapter 12

Bridge, *Vengeance*
Apogee: 37 Gem System
Local Date: C12/D20
Local Time: 1/8:00

As she watched the crew run through their preparations from her position on the bridge, Deidra knew she had made the right decision to join the mission.

Gregor had argued with her because of course he would.

He felt they couldn't afford to lose Deidra if anything went wrong. She understood that fear, and maybe even agreed with it. No one else was ready to take the reins if she fell. Martin Scalese, maybe, but even he had issues, not the least being that his background with intelligence would erode public confidence.

People need to feel heard, not watched.

But she understood the situation better than Gregor did.

"My father would have gone, too," she'd said. *"You know that's true. The people need to see me on board with them. And beyond that, you know what this mission is about. I'm not going to make someone else do my job."*

This mission to the Solar System would set the future direction of the Universe Three civilization as they knew it. She couldn't huddle in the protection of Apogee's invisible anonymity. She wasn't about to leave *Vengeance's* crew to run this operation without her.

She thought about that conversation with Gregor as she wrapped her hands around the rail of the upper deck encircling the bridge, and as she peered down to watch Captain Keyes command the flurry of activities that were prejump preparations.

He was, Deidra thought, exceptionally good at his job.

An air of electricity snapped across the room.

Keyes slipped from station to station as each technician put their computer systems through standard checklists and as each system command reported their readiness. She watched him lay a gentle hand on the shoulder of the shipboard system command station, and simply lock eyes with another crewmember. He knew these people. The crew was equally marvelous. Professional. Crisp. It was a crew that had been to war with each other. Even the four security officers standing guard in the wings felt dialed in and part of the team.

Vengeance was the obvious choice to run the mission.

They had *Defender*, too, but the decision to send *Vengeance* would have been unanimous even if Keyes hadn't personally requested the assignment. Universe Three had built the ship. It was their first self-made Star Drive spacecraft. If there was a vessel preordained to complete the mission to embed a black hole gate into Sol, *Vengeance* was that ship.

Her gaze went to the nav station — her role in the earliest years. Navigation.

It was where Deidra had first learned the discipline it took to make complex things happen. As a navigation officer she made her first ties with Katriana Martinez, and there that she first began to grow up. She wondered where she would be if her father had assigned her to any other role as she was starting out.

Life is like that.

Who could tell?

All she knew is that she would be a different person today. No better or no worse, but different. Seeing the operator walking through the checklists and verifying their coordinates made her hands itch, though.

She wanted to be doing something.

Something beyond thinking about the importance of the command she was going to soon give, anyway. A command that, if the mission were successful, would potentially go down in history as the most bloodthirsty directive given in all of human history — the command to attach the Solar System's sun to a massive back hole, hence put some thirty billion human lives into peril.

This was why she was here.

Why she'd fought Gregor so hard.

Deidra Francis had come by her reputation as a fanatical leader honestly. She'd given her life to the safety of the people of Universe Three, and if that meant she might go down in history as the woman who destroyed the Solar System, she could handle it. It was her call. Her legacy. She wasn't going to shackle the scientists who devised the tools with the baggage that came with their use.

She gripped the rail harder and stared out the view screen where their 37 Gem home star blazed away.

"Are you all right, Director?"

It was Allie Feder, who had come to stand at the rail beside Deidra.

Feder was aboard *Vengeance* for the same reason Gregor had pressured Deidra to stay behind — Universe Three couldn't afford to lose both of their top physicists on an errant mission. Though Catazara had made a show of promoting Feder for her work on the remote connection and she could now claim the title of full professor, as the junior member of the team Feder was considered by most to be the most expendable.

Like Deidra, the young physicist wore an unadorned U3 jumper as a uniform.

The dark green of the collar complemented the bronzy red of her hair. The long fingers of her hands, like Deidra's, wrapped around the sleek rail.

It was already clear that the young woman was going to play a part in U3's future, so it had been on Deidra's list of "things to do" to sit down with the young physicist and learn more about her. Now would be as good of a time to start as any.

"Yes, Professor," Deidra said. "I'm fine."

"Allie," Feder said. "I don't think I can't deal with that kind of formality right now, and my friends just call me Allie."

"All right, Allie. I'm fine. I was just thinking, is all."

"What about?"

"About how you're really going to have to get used to being

called professor."

Feder laughed. "I'm sorry," she said.

"It's all right," Deidra replied, chuckling first, then giving a wistful sigh. "About friends, I guess," she said, then noting confusion on Allie's face, added, "I guess I'm just sentimental in my old age."

"You're not that old," Allie said.

"That's what you say when someone is getting old," Deidra responded.

Feder's face went pale. "I'm so sorry," she said. "I didn't mean to—"

Deidra waved the rest of her response away.

"You don't have to apologize," she said. "I'm just annoyed because there's nothing for me to do until we get going."

"Well, that I understand."

Deidra recognized the younger woman's anxiety. She gazed toward the 37 Gem star again.

Feder's gaze followed. "It feels weird sometimes, doesn't it?" the physicist said.

"What do you mean?"

"37 Geminorum is just like Sol, isn't it? A classic G-type main-sequence star, just sitting there in the middle of space converting helium to hydrogen."

"Sol is smaller," Deidra said

Feder shrugged. "Only a little smaller."

"I suppose." She remembered a day before they'd settled on coming to Apogee when Kazima Yamada had estimated 37 Gem was older than the Earth's sun by a billion years or so and said that its metallicity suggested iron and ore would be plentiful in the system, a fact that had made it viable for them to call the system home. *It's like Sol, only different*, Yamada had said.

Deidra's thoughts went to the star, then. 37 Gem rotated every twenty-five days, and burned a bit brighter than Sol, its surface temperature at something over 6,000 degrees Kelvin.

"Sixty-sixty, twenty-five," she said aloud.

"Sixty-sixty, twenty-five?"

"37 Gem's surface temperature is 6,060 degrees K. It rotates every twenty-five days."

"Five-seven," Feder replied.

Deidra waited.

"As in, Sol is fifty-seven light years from us."

"I see."

"I remember it that way because my brother was seven when he died, and I was five."

"Hmm," Deidra replied, nodding.

Deidra had read reports. Feder's family had died in UG's raid on Atropos. Thinking about it reminded her of Kel Melody, then Jamal.

"It seems we all lost a lot on Atropos."

Feder pressed her lips together and seemed to stand straighter. "Sometimes," she said, "when the sky is clear at night, I go outside to look for it. Sol is close enough you can see it with the naked eye if you know just where to look."

"I do that sometimes, too."

Feder's low *hmm* of a response was light enough it made Deidra feel better. "If we can see them, they can see us, you know?"

Deidra nodded.

Fifty-seven light years meant she was seeing light created before she was born, created when her father and her mother were only just beginning their relationship. The movement was in its infant stages then.

What would they think of this conversation?

She looked at Allie Feder then and saw the weight on her shoulders.

Vengeance's mission was to put a black hole into Sol, and for all Deidra's bluster about taking the brunt of the decision, she couldn't change the fact that all this was built on the physicist's work.

"Are *you* all right?" she said.

"I'm fine."

Deidra turned to face Feder more fully. "It's a lot of responsibility, isn't it? To be such a young person with so much power?"

"I don't have any power."

"Bullshit."

Shock crossed Feder's expression. "Professor Catazara still—"

"Bull. Shit."

This time Deidra saw a level of truth inside that shocked expression.

Feder understood the power Deidra was referring to, but she

wasn't yet comfortable with it. She would be soon, with the right guidance anyway, but for now she felt that power and didn't know what to do with it. So, Allie Feder was the smartest person in the room, and yet, like Deidra, she too had been standing alone at the rail without anything to do.

Her time was coming, though.

Deidra put her hand on Feder's arm.

"It's going to be okay," Deidra said. "I was once too young for my position, too. Jorge will always be Jorge. I understand that. But you're the one making your way now. And don't think it's been lost on me that you're attending more and more sessions for him, and that in those few sessions he does attend he's deferring to you more often than not. I think you're going to be a very important person for us, Allie Feder. I'm sure you'll make mistakes. But that's okay."

Feder's lips relaxed gently. She ran a hand through her hair.

"Thank you, Director."

"Deidra," Deidra replied, smiling. "My friends call me Deidra."

"All right," Feder said, blushing.

Deidra waited, then cocked a questioning brow. "All right...?"

"All right, Deidra," Feder said.

The captain's voice broke in, coming across the communications system.

"Take launch positions."

Deidra turned to the row of padded seats alongside the command station.

"Shall we," she said to Allie.

"I'm sorry. I need to be on the system floor to engage the dimension drills and set the triangulators," Feder said.

Deidra laughed, this time with more irony than lightheartedness.

"Of course you do," she said, shooing Feder away as she took her seat.

"Thank you for this," Feder said.

"You're welcome, Allie," Deidra replied. She settled into the seat and, wanting the younger woman to relax, responded with the phrase that — given the aural display that jump travel created — had turned into a traditional prejump salutation among U3 crewmembers.

"Enjoy the show," she said.
"I will, Director."
Then she was gone.

Chapter 13

Bridge, *Vengeance*
Apogee: 37 Gem System
Local Date: C12/D20
Local Time: 1/8:14

Captain Keyes made a last pass through the stations, then came off the floor to stand next to the command station. The expanse of the bridge grew to a silence that still sparked with energy.

Operators and mission specialists turned toward the captain.

Keyes turned his gaze to Deidra, who gave a confirming nod.

"Mechanics?" Keyes said.

"We're good to go, Captain."

"System stability?"

"All systems locked in and safe for jump, Captain."

"Navigation?"

"Coordinates confirmed."

Hearing the conversation gave Deidra a warm feeling. Given her area of expertise, she'd been part of the group that had devised the exact plan for the jump and had even helped work out the coordinates they'd need to hit.

The process was going to be tricky.

The goal was to use Mercury as a blind to avoid detection for as long as possible. Given the current configuration of planets, a signal would travel to Venus Station in just under three minutes, to Earth in seven. A U3 raid had knocked Venus Station offline months earlier, but reports were that it was functional again — though would be of limited ability, and short-staffed for at least another standard year.

Surprise was on their side, but every minute they stayed in the Solar System was a minute the pendulum could slide in the other direction. Everyone on board understood how quickly the UG could react if they had resources available. Launching the pods to link to the black hole itself was a quick process, but not so quick that they could afford for the UG to discover them immediately upon arrival.

Put it all together and the jump envelope had to be very tight.

The closer to Mercury they could get, the better. But too close and they could have a disaster in multiple ways, not the least of which could be arriving in the same physical space as the planet itself.

It was that possibility that Gregor used to argue that Deidra really *should* remain home on Apogee, but it was a possibility she ignored.

Every jump could go wrong.

But Deidra had learned from the best. She knew how to build a navigation plan, and she wasn't going to stay on the sidelines while the image of Katriana Martinez weighed on her mind.

Keyes settled into his captain's chair, then glanced again at Deidra.

"Director?"

With one hand, she gestured he should continue.

"Crewmates," he said. "We are good to commence star jump. Enjoy the show."

THE MERCURY GAMBIT

Chapter 14

Vengeance, Mercury, Sun Side
Local Date: Undefined
Local Time: Undefined

Sitting at her station on the system floor, Allie Feder let her fingertips play at the edge of the angled panel where various readouts flashed their status. The edge was cool and rounded, hard against her flesh. The muscles in her leg quivered. Her palms were damp as she rubbed them against her pant legs. The anxiety that burned at the pit of Allie Feder's stomach was so sour and her sense of dread so deep that, when *Vengeance* came out of its jump, she could not remember the light show at all.

They arrived at their destination with pinpoint accuracy.

The spacecraft had tucked itself deeply into the shadow of tiny Mercury, locked in place, the planet and the spaceship now racing around the sun at a breakneck pace.

The nav station confirmed the crew had executed the jump plan perfectly. *Vengeance* flew with the proper vector and velocity that would allow the ship to stay in the shadows for as long as necessary. There were the expected adjustments to be made, retros to fire, trims to trim to avoid losing their position, but it was only a matter of a few minutes until *Vengeance* was stable.

Then it would be her turn.

As the time grew near, the pressure of being watched washed

over her. It was the crew, she realized, the eyes of her crewmates, filled with their own anxieties born of being as deep into UG territory as they could be, and born with the understanding of what this mission meant to their home. Director Francis could take the burden of her command, but every gaze in the room understood the full truth.

Desperate times call for desperate measures: Live or die, this was her mission.

A scant few moments later, the time came.

"Director Francis," Captain Keyes said, "the conn is yours."

As the director took a center position on the command podium, Allie breathed deeply and tried to appear collected, tried to recall the calming glance of Captain Shudar as they'd spoken before the test flight.

She wished U3 had given this mission to *Defender*, but she understood even at the onset of conversation that Captain Keyes would have his way with this decision.

So, she'd simply worked hard to prepare.

Allie had prepped the pods herself preflight.

They were ready.

Director Francis scanned the room, bringing everyone's gaze to hers. She steadied herself by placing the fingertips of both hands to the surrounding rail, then turned her attention to Feder.

"Engineering, please load the pods," she said.

"Pods loading," the response came through the ship's intercom.

Though Engineering Bay was far from the bridge, Allie could imagine the moment. Mechanisms grinding. Pods sliding into launch tubes. She imagined the clang of the caps and compression noises of air locks as the tubes themselves opened to space.

"Three pods ready for launch."

The director looked her way.

Allie took a glance at the datascreen projected before her.

The systems were properly powered. Coordinates proper.

It looked good.

"Prelaunch configurations confirmed, Director," she said.

"You are approved to launch, Engineering," Director Francis said.

"Aye, pod launch sequence begun."

A tracking projection hologram appeared in the center of the assembly room — complete with topographical representation of Mercury, *Vengeance*, and the position of the sun.

"*Pods are away.*"

Three pods glowed red as they separated from *Vengeance*.

They still had distance to travel.

Unlike the test process — but simpatico with the first ever wormhole missions — the three pods needed to breach the sun as part of their mission. But unlike the original wormhole pods that the United Government had deployed to set the gate in Alpha Centauri A, these three would serve their purposes in the upper regions of the star's construction, setting the triangulation zone in the corona such that U3 operators back home could drill the remote gate tied to the wormhole properly into the star's core.

The three would burn up eventually, of course. But that should be the only sacrifice made.

Allie waited, eyes scanning the readouts to ensure the three systems were still operational.

A moment later, three indicators appeared on the projection — one beside each pod.

They rolled through diagnostic code, then the dots flashed to white — and the three white dots represented on the map sped toward the solar corona.

They were good.

She took a very deep breath.

"Systems intact, Director," she said, locking eyes with Francis. "The launch is successful."

The room cheered, then, and Allie felt weight lift. The process should take something upward of a half hour, so best case was thirty minutes on site, then a jump back home. If the process completed properly, Catazara would have the remote gate set before they returned to Apogee.

"Nothing to do now but wait," Keyes said.

Great, Allie thought. *Exactly what I'm so good at.*

Chapter 15

"What the hell is that?" Remy de Victory said, staring at the 3-D holo field. A signal flared there, buried in Mercury's shadow, a cloud of noise that, at first, he'd felt more than seen.

He adjusted a set of switches, trying to add gain, then nudged a slider to first expand and then contract the incident angle.

"Probably just a spike," Gwenny Madrigal said after she slid her station closer. "I told you not to screw with anything."

"Don't start with me now, all right?"

The two had been more than friends when they first came to the station — and, in fact, that they were a couple was why they had chosen to take this very assignment. The job itself was interesting, though simple — watching over the complex bank of machines as they gathered their shit-tons of data and sent them to an equally large group of labs. They were both top students, both likely to use the kind of responsibility that came with working a science station as "kids" to springboard themselves to another way post. And, of course, their extra time allowed for other activities.

But that was six months ago, and when you're twenty-two standards old and things go wrong, six months can feel like forever.

That's what Remy would say later, anyway.

Now all he wanted to do was to get the hell done with this assignment and find a place back home in the asteroids.

He kicked himself for having said anything to her at all.

Why couldn't he have waited the fifteen minutes it would have taken for their shift overlap to be over, and she'd have been off duty? Speaking his thoughts was his thing, though. If something hit his brain it came out of his mouth. At the beginning of their time together Gwenny had found it an endearing quality. Now she just sat there in her chair, the braided strands of her hair dangling in the station's weak anti-g environment as she stared with those brown eyes into a projector readout.

The cloud was so weak he almost dismissed it, but the longer he took it in, the more firm is seemed to grow.

That was another thing she'd found attractive about him at first. He was sensitive to the environment around him and had an uncanny ability to take in situations and understand their meaning. It was a strange combination of senses and intuition — not quite touch, not quite vision. It had been a problem throughout his life, though. He jumped at things others didn't, for example, which made him weird to other kids. And he'd make predictions so spot on they thought he was spooky. It was only as he got through school that he realized this thing that was so normal to him was something others didn't have, and that it gave him certain advantages to go with those other discomforts.

It was a trait that made him so good at his job, which was as a system operator on this ramshackle dump of a science station out in the intersection of nothing and nowhere.

The edge of the signal had seemed to pulse at the edge of his vision.

He couldn't have missed it if he tried.

When Remy squinted more closely, he realized something was there.

Something big. Something churning power.

He pushed another gain lever a notch up to see if he could get the signal to coalesce better. The display was messy enough that Gwenny *could* still be right — it could be just a spike — but, first, he didn't think so, and second, he didn't need to be told what he should think, better yet be told by someone who — goddamn it — still smelled so good after an entire shift.

"Do you want me to kick the ShRA back to baseline?" Gwenny said, pronouncing it as *shrah* — one word.

"No," Remy said too sharply.

ShRA meant Solar-hard Radio Array, of which Venus Station had ten, each set to capture data with a 60x60-degree field of view and arranged in such a way that meant the station could sense any radio signal that hit it from almost any direction. He'd been playing with them to see if he could fix a hole created by the recent loss of the Gradient Array.

Debris damage was something the recruiter hadn't talked about in their pitch. It happened all the damned time, though.

The rebuild needed after Universe Three had disabled the station had progressed well enough, but the field of tumbling crap the attack had left behind in Venus's orbit was all over the place. It seemed like some system someplace was always picking up a shred of old fuselage, or a spinning bolt, or ... pick your poison.

Fixing shit turned out to be a major part of the job.

He'd come on duty today just like he'd done every other day — having just finished his post-breakfast workout, so he still felt the endorphin spike all through his body, and his brain was pleasantly dialed in after listening to slash-pop he'd dropped directly to his dataclip. He'd done all the system scans and run the standard checklists, noted that the power systems were fully operational, that the memory processors were active and storing, and the sensor arrays were on total readiness — except, of course, for that Gradient Array which had been trashed by space debris last week.

The Gradient Array was an important part of the system, though — a piece designed to pull high and low spectrum signals from space, then do a matching process with noise profiles that rode in waves of quantum foam. This matching resulted in a series of "gradient waves" that some high-brained scientists said might allow them, among other things, to see Star Drive jumps from afar.

It was too deep for him, really.

His brain could manage quantum stuff, but time dilation and space warpage built into multidimensional partitions froze his core.

What he understood completely, though, was that the Gradient Array going down was a major pain in the ass because, once whatever microparticle had struck it, his workload had doubled. Covering that ground now required recalibrating and rerouting a

ShRA to take its place. Given the rotation of Venus Station, the operator had to swap between two units every fourteen minutes and twenty-five seconds to keep from blowing out the receiver as it rotated toward the sun.

To make matters worse, the manual process didn't really capture all the data, either.

A ShRA was a cool piece of metal, great for reading classical radiation over the standard spectrum of X-ray, microwave, and gamma releases, but it had shit for brains when it came to quantum matching.

So, yes. A total pain in the ass.

His birthday was coming up soon. If he could wish for one thing besides a miracle that shortened his assignment, it would be to get the Gradient Array fixed so he could go back to the otherwise sleepy job of avoiding Gwenny Madrigal.

As a result of his disquiet, however, a couple of days ago he'd hacked together an automated timer to control the swap. It worked well enough but had failed when an unexpected coronal mass — was there any other kind? — fried the secondary processor he'd used to connect the various ShRA systems together.

So, it was back to manual.

And back to bitching about interrupting full episodes of *Keeping Faith* every fifteen minutes, a show he'd gotten into because Gwenny said she loved it, and that he kept taking in now because it was so good that even a sorry-assed breakup couldn't keep him away.

He had another idea while working out this morning.

He could adjust the scan range of the ShRAs' sensors by removing a filter that cut noise of the signals that bounced off the cloud of debris surrounding the station — then, rather than filter the input, use a dynamic algorithm to calculate the most likely angle of incidence that each signal had come from relative to the debris field — effectively using that debris like a giant fractured mirror, and thereby increasing the field of view each ShRA could take information from.

If that worked, he could pull at least one ShRA off the grid and dedicate it fulltime to almost replace the Gradient Array.

It was such an exciting idea he'd started working on it the moment he finished with the routine checks at the beginning of his shift. Now the prototype was in, but it wasn't working. The noise field was too hard to calculate.

Still, there was that thing that had showed up in the shadow of Mercury.

He reset the program, wondering if it was a remnant of his code. Still, the mass in the display remained. He felt Gwenny's attention shift toward the signal. She came to his station and leaned over his shoulder so close that the soft essence of her aura flowed over him.

"That's really weird," she said.

"Yeah. There's something there," he replied, adjusting the algorithm to let his code focus on incidence angles that held the most similarity. The cloud grew denser.

There was most definitely something there.

He dropped his program into two more ShRA systems and a moment later the signal grew even stronger.

"Is that a ship?" Gwenny said.

"I think it has to be."

A moment later he *knew* it was a ship.

He'd seen that signature before.

A Star Drive.

A Star Drive, tucked in behind Mercury.

The idea sent a spike of fear to pool in the pit of his stomach.

It didn't seem right.

What was a Star Drive spacecraft doing hiding behind Mercury?

He toggled the comm port.

"Abke," Remy de Victory said. "Patch me into Central Comms. I need to report a signal."

Chapter 16

Vengeance, Mercury orbit
Local Date: Undefined
Local Time: Undefined

Allie Feder held her breath.

Hovering above, at the focus of the bridge projection display, the three white holographic markers that represented the drill pods faded into the sun.

Her life flashed before her eyes — all the parts that mattered anyway. The studying, the contemplating, the dealing with an intellectual community that even now worked against youth. The focus she'd brought on tech, the time spent simply thinking about the world, gazing at equations until they made her eyes bleed.

Time stood still.

She remembered the smell of stale coffee. Flashed on faces of her mother and father. Her brother, still such a kid when he'd been taken from her. She lingered on possibility as she stared at the three places where the pods had disappeared, thinking that she could still see them, but knowing that was simply a case of phantom senses.

What if, she kept thinking. What would Benny have become if the United Government had allowed him to grow up?

The pods were all away — each past the transition zone of the sun's corona, into chromosphere and then its photosphere, dealing with all the other environmental crap that she no longer cared to

think about.
>It all came down to this moment.
>Would the tensors hold?
>Would the links be set?
>The wait was agonizing.

MACHINES

In the vastness of space three machines, launched from the belly of a human-built spacecraft, approach a standard G-type star.

Thermal sensors built into their bodies register rapid increases.

The superheated regions of the corona are the first suggestions of the hell that lies below. Frictional drag builds as the density of their environment increases from near vacuum to certain death.

Magnetic field generators the human creators have embedded into the body of the machines keep the first layers of the star's defenses at bay. But the machines continue on the doomed paths which, too, were programmed by those same creators.

Layers of heat-resistant composite char and crack.

Flames fold across the noses of each of the three machines as they slice deeper into the star's mass, trailing wakes of gaseous plasma as they fly onward.

Inside the machines, under multiple layers of those same composites burning their own existence away to protect the greater good, other machines come awake, initiating coded algorithms that toggle other algorithms, making adjustments to yaw and roll, driving the machines onto more pristine paths, deeper, crashing through the corona, shedding more layers of heat-retardant armor, boiling, searing — material flying away in explosive microparticles, atoms dissipating into photons and particles, their heavy metals adding infinitesimally to the star's metallicity that before then had been created only by the physics of God.

The transition zone sees final code toggle.

Unlike other pods before them, these machines do not need to reach the core to perform their assigned duties.

Fine-tuned masses collect inside the reinforced chambers in each machine, reach through dimensions that no human being has ever seen, linking together, forming a construct, a map through space and time.

Mathematics play out.

Impervious to the fire and the heat of even a thousand stars, physics forms a new foundation.

Then the machines are finished.

Gone.

Each erupting in an explosion, powerful, yet so inconsequential they fail to register on the sensors of any life form that has ever existed.

There is nothing to mark the moment as monumental, yet it is a point in history that can never be removed.

At a distance across the vastness of space, connected to the existence of the three machines, another algorithm toggles.

Waves ripple. Space folds.

A distant black hole, ravenous and cold, begins to feed.

CHAPTER 17

Vengeance, Mercury orbit
Local Date: Undefined
Local Time: Undefined

Agonizing seconds passed before the mission specialist toggled his earpiece.

"Primary tracking signal lost, Captain. Mission is complete."

"The tensor nodes?" Keyes asked the only question that mattered.

"Affirmative, Captain. Strong and firm. Target gates are set."

A cheer rose, loud and strong, and clapping and hugging commenced.

The vise grip that had been clamped on Allie's chest gave way with one single release. Tears came then, tears that were frightfully embarrassing but impossible to hold back.

No one seemed to mind.

Someone hugged her.

After years of conflict, after so many people dying, after years of jump-and-dash attacks that exposed them to dangers the crew knew were more than theoretical, these people understood what this moment meant for Universe Three.

Freedom. Safety.

Across the way, Deidra Francis beamed.

"All right, people!" It was Captain Keyes, voice booming to

gather his crew again. "We need to get home."

The admonition worked, though it was another half minute before the bridge was back to their stations and a new calm came over them.

"Prepare engines," Keyes commanded.

"Engines prepared."

Keyes moved down the line, ensuring all systems were prepared for their return.

"Navigation," he made the final call. "Jump coordinates set?"

Before the navigation station could answer, though, the ship gave a firm lurch, and the pealing blare of a klaxon split the air.

A bank of red lights pulsed with each peal.

"Captain," the systems commander said, "we have a breach!"

Chapter 18

Vengeance, Mercury orbit
Local Date: Undefined
Local Time: Undefined

Deidra Francis's stomach knotted as the klaxon blared.

She pushed herself out of her chair and grabbed the rail as she tried to gather information. Below her, the crew was a pit of action.

The holographic projection of Mercury rotated around their position in midair as red light pulsed around it.

"We have a visitor, Captain," the operator of the sensor station reported with professional calm that belied stress. "Enemy spacecraft inside Mercury orbit. UG, sir. Star Drive."

A new indicator, tinted blue, formed on the holoprojection — a single mass positioned in space close to their own.

Deidra's jaw clenched and her chest constricted.

"Damage reports, sir. Delta Deck reports a breach to vacuum," system command said.

"What the hell?" Captain Keyes said, obviously as shocked as Deidra was. They'd been so close to finished. Now this.

"Can we still jump?" Deidra called.

Keyes gritted his teeth. His gaze danced from station to station as he took in the situation. His eyes locked with the director's, and Deidre had her answer.

No. We cannot jump.

The captain beckoned to the closest young security officer who had, until now, been on standby.

"Get Director Francis to a pod," he commanded.

The guard, a fit young man, moved to take Deidra by the arm.

"You will do no such thing," Deidra replied, stepping away from their advances.

"Now!" the captain called, turning back to deal with this emergency.

"Come on, Director Francis." The guard spoke firmly, taking her again by the elbow as if to escort her out, but Deidra wrenched her arm and moved even further away.

"I'm not leaving this bridge."

"Deidra?" It was Allie Feder. She'd moved from her station and was standing beside her now, putting her hand on Deidra's shoulder. "The captain is right. You can't help anything here. We have to get you someplace safe."

It was the tone of Feder's voice that moved her more than her words.

She was right.

The scenario playing out on the projector was not good.

The captain was doing his proper duty in getting Deidra to a place of protection. She understood that. A UG craft jumping in meant trouble, and without the ability to jump, *Vengeance* was a sitting duck. If the damage could not be repaired quickly, things could get very ugly very soon.

Deidra glanced at the projector, which still displayed the topographic landscape of tiny Mercury.

She took in the fear etched on Feder's face, and in that instant knew Gregor Anderson had been wrong about something important: Universe Three would find a way to do without Deidra but it needed the physicist.

That was her job now — keep Allie Feder alive.

"All right," Deidra said, taking Allie Feder's arm. "But you're coming with me."

She pointed the security officer forward.

"Let's go."

BATTLE

Chapter 19

Apogee: 37 Gem System
Local Date: C12/D20
Local Time: 1/8:47

The cold, dry air of the communications center cut into Gregor Anderson's thin skin. He pulled his jacket collar up close to his throat as he guided his hover chair into Universe Three's primary data control room, but it did nothing to help. He hated this place — always bone cold to keep the entanglement links at the low temperatures they needed to manage universal communications. Luckily, this was the only place he needed to go where the environment was so harsh.

He didn't really want to be here.

He hadn't thought the mission was a good idea to begin with, and then — when Deidra had put her foot down and decided to go on it anyway — decided it was an astronomically bad one.

He had lost that fight, as he'd known he would. Deidra Francis came by her stubborn streak honestly. She was like her father before her.

Now he was here for the same reason everyone else was.

He needed to know.

"What's the word?" he grunted as he stopped the hover chair beside Martin Scalese's station, which sat on a stage-like platform raised a half flight from the operation's floor — a configuration that made it feel like they were surfing on a frozen wave. He wasn't surprised to see Professor Catazara and a group of six of his acolytes gathered together in one corner along with a few of the director's staff. Assuming mission success, Catazara would flip a toggle here to enact the casting of the gate to the black hole.

The whole thing made Gregor anxious.

All this advanced science felt dark somehow. There were things, he thought, that human beings shouldn't do.

Keeping his gaze on the data panel across the room, Scalese gave a distracted laugh that was no more than a faint puff of air pushed through his nose. "Everything's good so far."

"Meaning we haven't heard anything."

"Meaning," he said, "all we can do is wait."

"Well, that's good for me," Gregor replied. "Waiting is all I seem to be good for anymore."

"Don't be so hard on yourself, Vice Director. You're a good man."

Gregor gave a gruff grunt from deep in his throat.

"Tell that to my knees and back," he replied. "Getting old is a bitch."

He pulled his jacket closer around his throat again, then gripped the ball of his walking stick and pressed it into the floor beside his hover chair. He didn't plan to stand, but found such isometrics relieved the ache in his knuckles and shoulders.

Scalese, his full attention focused on data readouts, simply shrugged.

Across the room, the data panel showed figures and symbols flashing green and blue against its dark background. A series of tables showed system status. A steady flow of operational reports rolled down a wall panel.

Business as usual. So far.

Just another day in the park.

As if in response, three techs clipped into the system went about their work as if nothing special was happening.

The collection of equipment in the room made the place feel smaller than it was.

The block of systems that watched over the community's most important production facilities was spaced like columns along the wall to the left. Other comm channels entered the center though the roof, then ran in a collection of rounded guide trays along the ceiling, then fed into various convertors on the wall opposite. The entanglement core was a squat block of dark composite, two meters to a side, and another meter tall. Inside that block the most amazing physics known to humankind were playing out across dimensions, algorithms shifting and twisting to connect elements across galaxies in ways that Gregor had long ago decided to quit pretending he understood.

All that mattered was that the system connected to *Vengeance* in ways that let them read a few simple, but intensely important bits of data.

Its polished surface gave it a marbleized sheen that reminded Gregor of the benches in the middle of museums — squat areas for people to sit as they gazed at whatever marvels that curator had gathered.

Gregor gripped the head of his stick, feeling the tendons of his hand stretch.

Gregor could forgive Catazara and his acolytes for their focus, but he understood more was at stake now than the ability to set a wormhole pod. Technology always gets a second chance, but there was only one Deidra Francis.

She had surprised him. She'd grown up to become one of the finest leaders he had ever seen — including her father. And even if she didn't truly believe it, Gregor knew exactly how critical this moment was for the community. Universe Three was ready to expand, ready to colonize another settlement and become a real system of human beings who could work together in peace — ready to become, as Ellyn Parker had advocated, a true existence.

The memory of Perigee's speeches made him grin despite himself.

She'd been alone back then. Just one person with one idea that she sent blazing across her entire existence.

Look what she had accomplished.

The memory made his stomach tighten.

Despite Deidra's insistence otherwise, losing her could set Universe Three back decades, if not totally derail them.

Given Apogee's relative safety — protected by both distance and secrecy — he supposed it was natural that the young people of the day were getting soft.

Gregor was old school, though. He was of the generation who had faced the United Government head-on. He knew the enemy up close, knew it was still only a matter of time before they broke through. And, when they did, he knew Universe Three would need Deidra Francis.

Excited voices from the floor broke into Gregor's daydreams.

The techs, he realized.

Catazara's techs, suddenly whooping and squealing.

In the upper right quadrant of the display, the words *CONNECTION ACHIEVED* flashed in reddish-orange text.

One voice rose above the others.

"That's it! That's it! That's it!"

Then the techs were laughing and smiling and clapping each other on the shoulders and backs.

The professor himself remained stoic; his gaze focused on a different piece of the display. Noting their leader's concentration, the voices hushed, and all eyes went to that same section of the display.

Gregor had been to the briefings.

Once the three drillers had formed the guide-links, Catazara's technicians would toggle the algorithms to set the gate.

The display lit up.

The machines in Catazara's lab kicking into action...

TENSOR CALCULATIONS CONFIRMED.

...communicating across folded space-time with the three target-links...

CROSSCHECK INITIATED.

...modifying their multidimensional ballistics...

TARGET COORDINATES REFINED.

The professor's fingers wrapped more tightly into a ball as each hurdle was cleared.

Finally came the words: *CAST INITIATED.*

Then, seconds later: *TARGET ACTIVATED.*

The voices cheered with full-throated excitement. Technicians jumped and raised their hands over their heads. The staff members there — Yamada in particular — seemed to radiate with inner joy that can't come from anything less than a miracle achieved through years of hope and hard work.

The black hole gate had been set.

Sol was being drained.

The United Government now officially had A Real Problem to deal with, and Universe Three would soon be safe.

Even Gregor had to smile.

He turned his gaze toward the entanglement core, almost able to feel the wild speeds of calculations happening inside — or around — the solid black box.

He scanned the middle of the display that showed a data stream from *Vengeance* herself.

"Jump back," he muttered to himself, suddenly allowing himself to see that hope, almost willing now to believe they had pulled off the unimaginable.

Then the screen went suddenly blank.

Chapter 20

Vengeance, Mercury orbit
Local Date: Undefined
Local Time: Undefined

The UG attack continued.

The corridor lurched to the left, and Deidra crashed her shoulder into the wall. A moment later the artificial gravity system went off-line, and she, Allie Feder, and the guard were tumbling down the hallway in zero-g free float.

Warning beacons still blared, and the emergency strips flashed red and blue patterns.

Bad news.

Very bad news.

Her first thought flashed toward finding a service bay where they could grab a pair of magnetized boots, but that was a fool's game. This was no simple systemic malfunction. Her heart pounded, but just as she was feeling too out of sorts to function, the process-oriented section of her mind took over.

Everything seemed to slow down.

One step at a time, she thought.

And step one was to gain control of herself.

"Come on!" she yelled at Feder, and used the wall to push herself forward, shooting past the guard and ricocheting down the hallway. "Follow me!"

Getting to the loading bay meant riding a lift tube, which was farther down the corridor. The fact that lighting was still on meant the attack hadn't cut universal power, yet. They had to make it there before the system became inoperable, or they'd never make the pod bay.

Feder caught on quickly and flew through the open space behind Deidra.

Their security officer joined them, arms outstretched and legs working the walls, floor, and ceiling to keep going forward.

They reached the lift tube, and just as Deidra slammed the ball of her hand onto the sensor to call the lift itself, a clap of thunder filled the corridor. The walls shook with vibration, and the lighting system gave a loud snap. The hallway plunged into darkness punctuated only by the flashing emergency strips and the sound of the warning buzzer as it faded back into the room after the roar of the blast.

"We're dead," the man said.

That was right, she thought as she clung, panting, to a system box beside the lift tube.

Her hair floated around her face — as did Allie's.

Somehow the UG had figured out where they were and jumped a ship into the proper space. The mission must have been too rushed to have allowed them to coordinate target zones, which had kept them from destroying *Vengeance* on the first shot.

To survive a second was a minor miracle, too.

Vengeance would not make it through a third.

The lift tube was still working, though, and by wonders, the door opened.

"Is it going to hold?" Feder asked.

"It doesn't matter," Deidra replied. "Either we make it to the pod bay, or we don't."

The three of them pushed their way in.

"Shuttle loading bay," Deidra said.

The door slid shut and in darkness the ceiling crashed down on them as the tube began its descent. The guard gave a thick grunt as the barrier hit him flat in the back of his neck.

"Best be prepared for the stop," Feder said.

"If we make it that far," the guard said.

"Shut up," Deidra commanded, angry at herself even as she said it.

"I'm sorry, Director," the man replied.

They arrived at their destination a moment later, and all three managed to land safely as the door opened.

Normally expansive, a wall of black darkness now filled the shuttle bay.

Klaxons echoed in the cavernous space.

The aroma was thick with smoke.

CHAPTER 21

Apogee: 37 Gem System
Local Date: C12/D20
Local Time: 1/8:52

Gregor Anderson had long ago decided that there was only one advantage to growing old, and that was the propensity for others to dismiss him — and that this dismissal also made him invisible.

In the aftermath of *Vengeance*'s comm line going dark, the gathering was at first stunned into silence, then broke out in chattering that would make a family of baboons jealous.

Scalese's attempt to calm them down served only to add to the confusion.

Gregor was different, though.

He was ready.

He'd prepared for just this uncertainty.

Instead of panicking, as soon as the screen went dark, Gregor Anderson turned his hover chair around and left the communication room. He assumed no one would notice anything about his departure. Hell, he'd give even odds that no one would recall he had even been there.

This form of "fog of war" wouldn't last long, but it was his only weapon now.

With luck, it would be enough.

The air outside the communication center blasted him with a

wall of warmth that, despite his anxiety, he managed to savor.

He banked his hover chair toward the launch fields and pressed the throttle to full.

The sense of speed he felt was laughably low, but still the hiss of the engine made him feel giggly. Out of date or not, Gregor could still remember racing skimmers out in the open plains.

He focused on the moment, though.

There wasn't much time.

The staff would gather quickly, but without Deidra to corral them, they would argue about everything, hiding behind power games and political positions. Time was of the essence, but their haggling could well go on for hours.

Only when it was too late would they make any decision.

Gregor understood, though. He'd seen emergencies up close.

Something needed to be done, and it needed to be done now.

That's what he was thinking as the hover chair made its way down the road toward the launch fields, a gentle breeze pulling at his thin hair.

Though the hover chair was already at full speed, he pushed harder on the throttle.

The tiny engine gave a steady, high-pitched whine.

"Oh, Deidra," he muttered over the hum. "You should have listened to me."

"We've already lost *Icarus*," Kazima Yamada said. "If we've also lost *Vengeance*, I don't think we could withstand another."

"We can't leave her out there," Scalese replied for the fourth time.

As protocol demanded, the entire staff had come together for an emergency session.

"It wasn't supposed to happen this way," Deego Larsi said. "It was supposed to be in and out. A quick jump. What happened? Are we sure there's even a problem?"

"Like I said before," Scalese said, not even trying to keep the edge of desperation from his voice, "if *Vengeance* could jump it would already be in 37 Gem space, and if its comm stations were operational it's fair to say we'd know what was going on. The ship still shows up on our basic nav sensors as being in the Mercury shadow. So, yes, *something* is wrong."

"And that something could be anything from disaster to simple system failure, right?" Yamada challenged.

"You're suggesting that *Vengeance* could have both a communications problem and a Star Drive problem at the same time?"

"It's possible," she replied. "We've had multiple failures in mid-operation before. And if that's the case, we can't discount the danger of jumping another ship into the same coordinates that *Vengeance* ran. There's only so much space in Mercury's umbra. If we get that wrong, we risk both possible disaster of two ships in the same space and — more likely — drawing attention from UG at a time when *Vengeance* is obviously stranded."

Scalese sighed.

The entire room knew both positions were valid.

If *Vengeance* was in dire trouble, they could lose Director Francis and the whole crew.

They really should be safe, though. For the short term, anyway. Like Larsi said, it was supposed to be a quick in and out — and the blackhole gate was set, which proved the ship was intact at least up until that moment.

If they were simply dealing with a buggy system, jumping in would add to the risk.

They had to come to a consensus, though. And they weren't any closer to one now than they had been when they first filed in. Should they jump another ship to Mercury to come to *Vengeance*'s aid, or should they hold tight and avoid drawing attention to her while the crew made whatever repairs were necessary?

"What do you think, Gregor?" Scalese said.

His gaze flitted around the assembly, and suddenly he — and the whole collective, for that matter — realized the vice director was missing.

"Where the hell is he?" Scalese said.

Yamada shook her head and shrugged.

"I don't know. Probably taking a nap."

It had been a while since Gregor Anderson had piloted a skimmer — or, as the kids were calling them today, a trollycraft — but he knew he could still manage the basics. The ship was small with a small bit of a loading bay, designed for low orbit and used primarily to shuttle people or small cargo between the planet and larger spacecraft.

Deidra had wanted everyone in the Universe Three community to experience space travel, so security here was mostly unnecessary. Ride-along billets and other chartered trips were always available at limited notice. Guards controlled the area mostly to keep joy-minded kids away.

"Good morning, Vice Director," the gate monitor said as Anderson approached.

He flashed his credentials, and a gate swung open.

A moment later he'd guided the chair past the station and assigned himself a skimmer.

"I need to inspect a change that's been made in the forward Atmospheric Control system," he said to the steward. "I'll be back in a few hours."

The steward noted it and handed him a control chip.

Five minutes later he had the systems toggled on, and the takeoff boosters engaged. The little craft shuddered as it rose from the ground, rotated into position, and lifted its nose toward open space.

Gregor smiled, feeling vibration as the craft rose, sensing heat over the vehicle's shell even though he couldn't feel its full brunt.

The sensation of flying alone reminded him of his boy, Matt, long ago dead. His son had been a beautiful flyer. A born pilot. He'd given his life to the cause.

Like his own life would be, eventually.

Someday he hoped he'd see his boy again, but for now, sitting in a small skimmer and racing into Apogee's upper atmosphere was as close as he was able to get.

"*Defender*, this is Vice Director Anderson," Gregor said as the skimmer drew close enough that the features of the Star Drive came into view. "Please prepare a shuttle dock for me."

"Aye," the response came.

Chapter 22

Defender: Apogee orbit
Local Date: C12/D20
Local Time: 1/9:15

Commander Jessamine "Jess" Mikayla took a seat at a station beside Stephen Philo, who was the ship's communication officer. "Did the vice director give any indication why he's coming on board?" she asked.

The man shrugged. "Not a word."

Jess grimaced.

She didn't like surprises.

Especially when something big was going on — which there clearly was. Something big enough the captain said he hadn't been allowed to tell her about before going planetside.

She didn't have to be particularly sensitive to know the staff knew something was up, too. Everyone understood *Vengeance* had jumped, but beyond that information was tight.

The staff was good, though. Battle-hardened after years of running ops against UG positions. They'd gone about their business keeping the spacecraft ready, because that's what they did. There was no doubting there'd been an air running through the bridge all day, however. A sense of tension floating under their veneer. Something was going on, and the crew wore their anxiety in the same informal but professional way she wore her uniform —

which was in the more comfortable, informal fashion, jacket collar open to reveal the pine green sweater underneath.

She'd had her name "Jess" embroidered in the jacket's fabric because she wanted people to know it was okay to call her by that name rather than Jessamine — a three-syllable monstrosity that usually came out of other people's mouths as Jezz-a-mine, which she always thought sounded like Jezebel, which she hated.

She had been second-in-command for something over two standards now, and with Captain Shudar off-board for the impromptu staff session, *Defender* was under her command.

"Shouldn't Anderson be at the staff session, too?" she said to the communications officer.

Philo gave her one of his patented motions that was half nod, half shrug. They had come to know each other well since they had both been junior officers on the *Defender*, at least six standards ago.

She gave a soft grunt.

"You're not being much of a help."

Her stomach grumbled.

Why was it that she always got hungry before things went to hell?

Moments later, Gregor Anderson rode his hover chair onto *Defender*'s bridge.

"Welcome aboard, Vice Director," she said, rising from her seat and making her way toward the command level. "What can we do for you?"

"Prepare for jump," Anderson replied, his voice as gruff as his lined face and scraggly gray beard. "Coordinates as follows."

"I'm sorry, sir," Jess said as she climbed the last stair to the command podium. "But I'll need to contact Captain Shudar before we go jumping into space."

Anderson pounded the end of his walking stick onto the floor hard enough it rang. "There's no time for any pleasantries," he nearly screamed. "Any delay could result in the loss of *Vengeance*."

When no one moved, Gregor dismounted the hover chair, balanced carefully on his stick, and stood to whatever his full height was.

"I know your captain is surface-side," he said, wheezing now with big breaths, his cheeks growing more than ruddy red. "But I am Gregor Anderson, Vice Director of Universe Three. And when

I direct you to prepare for jump, you'd better damned well do it."

Jess stared at him for only the briefest of moments.

Her crew was well-trained. They would follow her command over the vice director's because that was the way the U3 system worked. This was her ship now. They were her crew.

Which meant she had calculations to make, calculations that might well change her career.

Gregor Anderson was a hero, yes, an icon in the U3 community.

But he was an old man, too, rumored to be more figurehead these days than a man who held any true power. Yet here he stood on her bridge, clearly in a state of extreme agitation, telling her that *Vengeance* could be at stake.

It was that last that made the call easy.

She wasn't going to be the officer who lost a Star Drive.

She turned to her crew.

"Navigation station, prepare to receive the vice director's coordinates," she commanded. "All other stations prepare for jump."

CHAPTER 23

Vengeance, Mercury orbit
Local Date: Undefined
Local Time: Undefined

Bleating klaxons grated the air inside the lift tube. The acrid scent of electrical fires grew as Deidra stared into the blackened depths of the cavernous shuttle bay.

Across its expanse, a bank of emergency lights flicked and flashed to cast gauzy clouds of light in the haze of the area.

The place was in chaos.

By directive, any operation made into UG territory required *Vengeance*'s crew keep its bay fully equipped and on alert to complete attack sorties with minimal preparation. Without the artificial grav system in operation anything not tied down — tools, people, and even spacecraft that were being prepped for launch — was now floating or flying or spinning in the midspace of the bay. A data panel crashed into the wall near the lift-tube opening. A sweater or shirt rippled with an unsettlingly macabre waveform that traveled up and down its fabric as it glided by. Loose components of plasma projectile systems clanged against the wall to their left.

To the right, a rack of rockets was strapped to the floor.

Her eyes adjusted, and Deidra saw the area strewn with other bits of smoldering equipment, and crew members already working to get them tethered. Between klaxon blares a cacophony of voices echoed in the area.

The control center loomed over the bay, a dark tower in a dark room. Its central office, built high to give it a full 360-degree view, flickered with the hauntingly spare blue and green aura of light from the few pieces of equipment that still worked within it.

They'd been hit hard.

Down the way, a row of XB-class fighter craft remained in a line, two of them with pilots in their cockpits had already been prepping for flight.

She grabbed the security escort.

"I'm taking one of those. Go tell the controller we need to get into the lock."

The air lock. The term seemed to finally land in the officer's mind. Deidra was going to take Allie Feder into space. Remove her from *Vengeance* to protect her in the now likely case that this attack would destroy the ship. It was a dangerous step — one that could leave them stranded if *Vengeance* was, indeed, lost. The loading bay's launch operations happened through a series of launch sections, each consisting of a series of air locks.

Deidra was going to use one now.

"Understood," the officer said, pushing himself toward the control tower.

Her eyes adjusted to the dim lighting. Ahead, Deidra saw the shape of a fighter.

Universe Three engineers had modified the XB class so often that it barely qualified anymore, but she wasn't here to argue specifics. It was a two-seater, disengaged from the loading bay floor, and floating peacefully in the zero-g environment. Two support technicians twisted in open space nearby, probably in process of preparing it for launch. It was more hopped up than she was prepared for. But beggars can't be choosers.

In the dim light, Deidra saw both cockpits loomed open, waiting for their pilots.

"Come on," she said to Feder, then pushed off the side of the lift tube to fly toward the spacecraft.

"Do you know how to fly that thing?"

Deidra ignored Feder's question, and concentrated on the rotation of the machine, trying to gauge what the ship's orientation would be when she arrived. A wing, she thought. She would grab on to one of the XB's stubby protuberances that served as wings once the craft hit atmosphere. It rolled into her range as she neared.

With one hand, she clasped the wing's edge.

Her body torqued to one side, and slammed into the XB's fuselage, but she held on.

From somewhere above her came a solid *whump*.

"Allie?" she called.

"I'm right here," Feder replied.

The mass of their bodies latching onto the craft made the XB lurch into a new orientation. The physicist clung there now, nursing what was likely at least a bruised shoulder.

"Get to the seat!" Deidra called, motioning at the copilot's back cockpit.

The fighter's momentum bounced it against the floor, but it remained intact.

With one hand still gripping the wing's edge, Deidra dug the fingertips of her opposite hand into a smooth depression built into the upper surface of the wing. That region added a touch of stability when the craft was in the upper regions of an atmosphere, and helped the wing shed heat while crossing more dense regions of reentry. Her fingertips slipped, but a dynamic material had been used as a liquid rivet at the bottom of the depression. Now that material held just enough of a variance with the metal around it that it helped her fingers keep contact.

She bent her knees against the spacecraft's body and, using her strong grip on the wing's edge, inched forward.

Her movement increased the ship's rotation.

For a moment, she thought her fingers might just rip apart trying to hold on so tight, but then the cockpit loomed above. She pushed off the wing with her knees, gently as she could, and grabbed the edge of the radiation-hardened glass that would — hopefully — soon cover the seat.

Clinging, she looked to the back.

Allie Feder held her shoulder awkwardly and, panting with exertion, was working to get into the seat.

"You good?"

"I'll get there," Feder grunted as she swung a leg into the cockpit.

Convinced Feder was going to make it, Deidra spun in zero-g

and slipped into the front seat.

She remembered once when she was young and Matt Anderson was pursuing her — *we'll make the perfect power couple!* she remembered him saying — that Matt had tried to impress her by taking her on a space ride full of acrobatics and dandy-doo. He hadn't realized that Deidra had been flying skimmers since she was old enough to walk and that she had graduated through the flight classes as she grew older. She still could recall the astonished expression on young Mr. Anderson's face when she took the controls, hit the trims, and flew a barrel roll with a dive eight. The memory gave her confidence now.

It had been decades since she'd flown for real, but she knew how.

She punched the communications system, then initiated prelaunch computer checks.

The display flashed on.

The hollow sounds of Feder making her way into the XB came as both audible grunts as well as distant vibrations through the spacecraft's framework.

Grabbing the helmet from its storage compartment to her left, Deidra crammed the thing onto her head and clipped into the system feed, happy to hear a radio burst.

"Plug in!" she screamed, hoping Feder would understand well enough how to do the same.

When Deidra toggled both cockpit controllers, the cowlings slid forward to enclose them both — and as they latched on, Deidra was surprised how the covering muffled the warning beacons and calmed the chaos around them.

The sound of her breathing rose, and she could feel herself thinking.

"Initiation complete," the system reported.

The cowling lit up with its control display.

Deidra fixated on the orientation of the craft's rotation — or wobbling would be a better term. The XB was going all sorts of ways. It was lucky they hadn't hit anything big, yet. But time was closing in, and the ship's sensor array was better than her eyes. She fired up the trim controls and used microbursts to get them stable.

"Wow," Allie's voice came from the system. "You really can fly this."

"Enough," Deidra replied, trying not to be annoyed.

She needed her concentration.

The XB was a souped-up machine. Yes, she could fly it, but it was just as possible she could shove it right up against the ceiling.

She rotated the trim boosters and edged the XB forward.

"Tower, I need a lock gate opened."

Nothing came from the tower.

"Tower," she called again, craning her head to see if there was any action inside. "Are you there, Tower?"

An earsplitting screech came from all around her, a monumental wall of sound, the wailing, piercing clang of a hammer driving into metal — and then that metal screaming with a thousand voices that sliced into her mind like knives.

Pitch darkness fell, and there was only the outline of the XB's sensor display showing the walls of the shuttle bay twisting before them.

Her brain raced.

A hit! The UG had hit them badly enough that huge chunks of *Vengeance*'s external shell were crumpling.

They had to get out, and they had to get out now.

She flipped on her weapon systems, hoping they'd arm, then banked into a turn her system said pointed the XB directly at a closed lock gate.

She would have to blast through.

The blast would breach the ship, but that was ordained.

Vengeance was done.

Unless she could do something, the people onboard were lost.

She felt the wall before them as if it were a live thing — an enemy looming in the darkness.

Engines engaged, she hit the throttle and the trigger on the XB's pulsed plasma cannon at the same time.

The beam flashed purple. The XB raced forward.

She triggered the cannon again.

Still the charred wall remained intact, flames flickering coldly at the edges of the wound Deidra had inflicted.

Acceleration pressing her body into the pilot's seat, Deidra Francis pulled the trigger one more time. Feder's scream merged with the roar of the XB's engines. The blast of plasma phasers thundered against the air-lock door, erupting into a plume of purple fire.

Flames of orange and violet engulfed the craft as it plunged blindly into that ball of fire — flashes of white so brilliant they might have blinded her. The sound of her engines roared, and the clatter of debris buffeted the fuselage.

Deidra fought the controls.

The craft thumped one way, then another.

A solid *thunk* came from the cowling above her, and Deidra was certain that the covering had to have shattered.

Then there was nothing.

Chapter 24

UGIS Hercules, Mercury orbit
Local Date: Undefined
Local Time: Undefined

"Abke," Jonas Rathpari, captain of the UGIS ship *Hercules* said. "Please connect me to Central Command. Admiral Umaro if she's available."

He was pleased with himself.

Pleased with his crew.

They had used complete surprise to their full advantage. The Universe Three ship *Vengeance* was, if not dead, completely derelict. His crew was free to pick the bones of the spaceship at their leisure.

At first, he thought this emergency mission was just another bullshit boondoggle of a device thrown his way to sidetrack *Hercules* from more important missions out hunting U3 where it lived. He was sure Command had been doing just that — hampering his ship's ability to succeed in lieu of other captains. In fact, he knew that had been true.

If they'd understood what was really happening, he doubted *Hercules* would have gotten the call despite being the craft most well positioned to meet the mission profile.

He could imagine the conversation at Central Command.

Odd signal in the halo of Mercury? Possible U3 sneak attack? Sure, riiight. Oh, I know, let's sic Rathpari on it. Won't that be a blast?

If that had happened, then at least *Hercules* was going to have the last laugh.

He scanned the display laid out before him.

The debris field would take a bit to settle down before it was safe to proceed, but the end was no longer in question.

"Central Command connected," Abke's voice came through.

A moment later, the face of Naomi Umaro filled the screen, every hair on her head, as always, perfectly in place.

"Greetings, Admiral," Rathpari said. "I have good news."

"Good news is always appreciated."

"We have engaged the Universe Three ship *Vengeance*. I'm pleased to say that it is no longer operational."

"That is good news, Captain," she said. "Congratulations."

"I will forward all mission profile data briefly," Rathpari said. "May I have your permission to run search and rescue on the enemy craft?"

"Yes, Captain Rathpari. You have that authorization."

"Thank you, Admiral."

"I look forward to the reports."

The connection rang off and an immense swell of satisfaction filled Rathpari.

Despite her efforts to hide it, he'd seen the expression on the admiral's face. She'd been surprised. Perhaps flummoxed. He was going to enjoy their first conversation when he brought *Hercules* back to port for her hero's welcome.

He was as certain of that as he was of the fact that there would be considerable search of *Vengeance*, but no rescue.

"Prepare the teams," Rathpari said. "But continue to fire on the vessel until those teams are ready. And launch Flare Squadron, too."

"Fighters, Captain?" his second-in-command asked. "Are you expecting trouble?"

"I've seen U3 up close before."

His second gave Rathpari a considered gaze but said nothing more.

It was a wise move, the captain thought.

Rathpari's comments had an edge that he hadn't been able to completely erase.

Rathpari was telling the truth when he said he had seen U3 before. He'd been visiting family on an Earth holiday leave when the terrorists flew their horrendous three-pass strafing missions. He'd been on stand in the asteroid belt when a coordinated U3 operation had destroyed hundreds of mining facilities. Both events had cost lives.

Too many lives.

Universe Three would pay for those lives now.

He had already spoken to the commander of Flare Squadron — who he knew as another officer with no love for terrorists.

When he was done, the U3 ship would no longer exist.

It was not his fault, Rathpari thought, that the Universe Three terrorists were so fanatical that they would fight to the last warrior.

That was a truth.

A certainty.

A fact that everyone should know and one that, when he was finished, everyone *would* know.

"All right, Captain," his second finally said. "I will relay your commands."

Chapter 25

XB fighter, Mercury orbit
Local Date: Undefined
Local Time: Undefined

The fighter emerged from the flames into darkness, and Deidra knew they were in the second stage. Rather than another air-lock gate, however, was a field of open space. *Vengeance* had been breached, its hull now a ragged maw of shattered teeth that yawned open to a distant star pattern.

She focused and flew, pointing the XB at the gaping hole, gripping the navigation yoke so hard she thought her hands would bleed.

The explosion that had ripped that huge hole into the hull had also left behind another sheet of debris that rattled off the XB's body — a shower of metal on metal that sounded like a frying pan on full sizzle.

If any of those got through the XB's hull, they were dead.

If an engine stalled.

If the flames were too hot. If...

Then they were through the lock and racing through space.

Below them the sun burned brightly, above and behind them the curve of Mercury's horizon cut through the darkness.

Deidra banked the XB back toward *Vengeance* to see the ship was still recognizable, but that it was now certainly derelict. Huge chunks of its body had been ripped to shreds. Shards of space garbage shimmered in prismatic clouds as they caught both the sun and Mercury's reflective light.

Behind her, Feder gasped.

"It gets worse," Deidra said, more calmly than she felt.

She had also checked the onboard radar signals, and the truth of what they were facing had already begun to settle in.

She turned the XB on its tail, and a moment later a ship appeared before them: UGIS Excelsior class Star Drive *Hercules*, its cannons flashing from both side-pods, its fire landing unmercifully on the remains of the U3 spaceship.

"My God," Feder said.

"Yes," Deidra replied. "My God."

It might have been a whisper or a prayer. A simple plea. A pledge of sorts. A benediction.

All Deidra knew at that point was that *Hercules* was not only destroying the U3 spaceship.

It was executing everyone on board.

Anger boiled inside Deidra's veins as *Hercules*'s guns flared again and again, ripping greater and greater chunks of flesh from *Vengeance*'s bones. Four. Six. Eight flashes of plasma torpedoes flared.

They didn't need to do that, she thought.

Vengeance was already dead in space.

Instinctively she engaged the full thruster and tilted the trims downward. The XB dove like a charm, but she felt her lack of experience as the craft overran her commands and only the strength of the restraints kept her from plastering herself into the cowling above the cockpit. Yes, she could fly the thing, but flying it and commanding it were two different questions.

"What are we doing?" Feder said, her voice strong enough to say she'd regained something of her composure.

"We're dead anyway," Deidra said, understanding now the full truth of that statement. Those shots meant *Hercules* was not taking prisoners. "But I'm not going alone."

The Excelsior Star Drive was a dangerous ship, but surprise was on her side.

Enough space crap was floating around — and enough residual radiation from the UG attack — that a single XB could lose itself in the noise.

If she could get below *Hercules*, come up on the underside where the bay doors opened, she could cause enough damage to keep its own XBs out of commission, or at least out of commission for long enough that she could fly a path to the Star Drive itself. At least then *Hercules* would be as dead of a duck as *Vengeance*.

She adjusted the spacecraft, feeling it move as she used feet, hand, and eye movements to chart a course.

She remembered her earliest days piloting, heard her father's voice.

Thruster for speed and direction, trims and particle pods for precision, he'd say over and over again. He never expected her to fly as a purpose, but knew it might be necessary someday, and wanted her to be prepared. That was a long time ago, though.

"All right, girl," she muttered to herself, glancing up through the scarred cowling to see *Hercules* coming into proper view. "It's time to get shit done."

She pulled up hard on the main.

Tripped a trim booster on the nose to keep it steady.

Only when the maneuver came around did she let herself reach for the plasma gun.

Her stomach dropped.

They were too late.

In the distance the bay door already gaped open, and a stream of UG fighters surged into space.

"We're screwed," she said.

"They don't see us!" Feder called.

She was right.

The fighters were deploying toward the *Vengeance* wreckage rather than chasing their XB. One pass, she thought. Whether they ran or not, it was only a matter of time before *Hercules*'s sensors would find them. But if the UG's *Hercules* kept its gaze on U3's *Vengeance* for long enough, she could get in one good pass.

Deidra turned the XB toward *Hercules*'s Star Drive engines.

Chapter 26

U3 Starship *Defender*: Mercury orbit
Local Date: Undefined
Local Time: Undefined

It was Gregor Anderson's worst case scenario.

Defender came out of the jump to find the shards of *Vengeance* strewn through space, and the UGIS *Hercules* on station, support craft already pouring into open space, fighters already mopping up the few remaining U3 craft.

At least he'd been prepared.

"Fire at the enemy ship, targets A and B," he called as more complete details of the situation registered on the holoprojector.

"Firing commencing."

He turned to the operations officer.

"Get me a readout of every compartment that remains of *Vengeance* that suggests life — electronic emissions, thermal profiles, erratic behavior. I want everything."

The officer seemed dazed.

Gregor wished he knew the woman's name so he could take her down a notch but also knew that wasn't of the utmost importance at this moment.

"Now!" he yelled.

The officer nodded.

"Cannons fired," reported the weapons officer. "Direct hit on portside weapons system."

"Starboard?" Gregor asked.

"Status uncertain."

"Continue to focus on Target B until it's certain. Once that's done, drop the Star Drive. We'll only have the advantage for a few more minutes."

"Do you want me to launch counterstrike fighters?" Commander Mikayla asked.

"Yes," Gregor said. "Focus on the fighters themselves. We don't know who might still be alive on board and we've got to protect the debris."

"Nothing against the Star Drive for now?"

"Perhaps a small sortie, just to occupy them."

"Yes, Director."

"Vice Director," he corrected the officer, his mind flashing to the internal debates he'd had ever since Deidra had decided to go.

"Yes, Vice Director," the commander replied, then got to her task.

Gregor drew a hard breath to calm his nerves, and finally collapsed back into his hover chair. The enormity of the moment draped him like a cloak. Until this moment, most considered his title to be ceremonial at best. Hearing himself called director brought the truth to him more fully than ever. If Deidra Francis was lost, the movement was done. There was literally no one to follow her. Gregor was old, and Deidra's brothers, Cash and Wallace, had never been close to capable. At best they'd get a committee of well-meaning but horribly lost bureaucrats who couldn't decide to piss if their backs were against a wall.

The bridge got busy then.

He breathed heavily and felt his heart pounding in his chest.

He was tired.

He was right when he said they'd have the advantage for only a few moments. *Hercules* would catch on quick enough, and beyond that, the UG would send more sharks as soon as they sensed blood in the water.

Vengeance was broken, and there was work to do.

Gregor ran his craggy hands over his eyes.

"Oh, Deidra," he muttered to himself. "Look what you've gone and done now."

Chapter 27

XB fighter, Mercury orbit
Local Date: Undefined
Local Time: Undefined

Deidra banked the XB hard into her run at *Hercules*'s Star Drive engines, feeling a sense of insane laughter as she blew past UG fighters on the way. She enjoyed the image of the UG pilots' astonished surprise as she flashed on their sensors, then outraged recognition as they saw a fellow XB-class fighter buzz their formations.

They thought they were alone out here.

How long would it take them to realize she wasn't one of them?

It didn't matter in the end. No one was coming for her, and she wasn't even sure if she wanted them to. Losing another ship in a valiant effort to salvage *Vengeance* would be throwing good money after bad. But that didn't mean she had to give up herself, and Deidra wanted this small victory. If she was going to die, she'd die doing damage.

The Star Drive engines lay just ahead.

Ten seconds was all she needed.

Five.

A flash of plasma from somewhere in deep space startled her. *What the...*

Then the cannon on *Hercules* portside disintegrated in a flash of energy.

Four.

Debris from the destroyed cannon clattered against the XB's hull. The main thruster shuddered, then went dead.

Three.

In free glide now, Deidra kept her focus. Her XB was dead. She wouldn't get another chance.

Two.

Hitting the Star Drive was all that mattered.

One.

She depressed the trigger, and released her own blast, the plasma flying straight and true into the system.

An explosion came.

Then the little XB fighter was spinning, derelict in space, rolling and tumbling awkwardly.

Headed straight for the surface of Mercury.

Chapter 28

UGIS Hercules, Mercury orbit
Local Date: Undefined
Local Time: Undefined

On the bridge, Captain Rathpari was livid.

The Universe Three ship *Defender* had arrived on the scene unexpectedly and gotten a shot off before his weapons systems could adjust their focus from *Vengeance*.

Warning klaxons blared. Blue lights flashed.

One cannon was gone, the other uncontrollable.

Now this.

"Star Drive system has been hit, Captain," the communications officer reported. "Status unknown, but jump engines are no longer available."

Rathpari pounded a fist into his armrest.

"That's impossible," he called.

"Fighters reporting a rogue XB-class craft in the area. Universe Three design."

"Where did it come from?"

"I'm not certain, Captain. It could have launched during the primary attacks and gotten lost in emissions."

Rathpari's heart pounded. The taste of loss nearly choked him, and for a moment his vision went red. This couldn't be happening. Reliant now on only relativistic engines, *Hercules* was derelict in the system. His two biggest weapons were offline, and his squadrons were all deployed.

They needed time to recover, or *Defender* was going to eat them for lunch.

They needed to get moving.

"Impulse engine full on, initiate Evasion Mars Maneuver," he commanded. The jink was a technique first tried during an earlier U3 attack and had been successful. It would leave the fighters isolated, but it was a gamble he needed to take.

"Should I report status to Central Command?" the comm officer asked.

"No," Rathpari responded. "This is our mission. I'll be damned if we're not going to finish it."

The idea of calling for help repulsed him. They'd already reported victory. To give that up tore at his guts. They could still win, too. He could counter off the Mars Maneuver and if that worked, he could cripple Universe Three beyond their ability to measure. If he could pull this off, he and his crew would be true heroes.

It wasn't too late.

"Divert all attack vectors to *Defender*," he said, feeling a fresh sense of bravado fill his body. "We've already blown one terrorist spaceship to bits, why not make it two?"

Chapter 29

U3 Starship *Defender*: Mercury orbit
Local Date: Undefined
Local Time: Undefined

Everyone on the bridge watched as the holo display showed the second explosion on *Hercules*.

"It's their Star Drive engines, Vice Director," a controller reported. "They've been shredded."

"How?" Gregor asked, standing up with his stilted movements to peer more closely at the display.

"No idea at present. But *Hercules* does appear defanged."

His knees and hips hurt in the artificial gravity, and his knuckles ached as he wrapped fingers around the captain's rail. But his heart still leaped into his throat. So much of war was about luck, but he couldn't believe they'd just gotten so lucky as to destroy one cannon, disable the other, *and* kill the Star Drive engines with what was essentially one salvo.

The image was clear, though.

Whatever the cause, there would be time to find it later.

Hercules was dead to rights, and if they could disable the fighters, they would have a brief window to run rescue operations without harassment.

"Well," he said. "Beggars should not be choosers."

Still standing, he scanned the faces around him.

"Flight Commander," he called. "All fighters engage with *Hercules*'s squadrons. Weapons Command: Full focus on that second cannon. When that's done, help pick off the fighters."

"On it."

"Commander." Gregor turned to Mikayla. "Prepare for search and rescue operations."

The commander looked like she was going to suggest an alternate idea.

"Now!" he said. "Timing will be everything."

"Yes, sir," Commander Mikayla replied.

As he spoke, a flash of light flared against the observation screen. A rumbling sound came through the craft.

It was nothing special — a fighter strafing run and a lucky shot at best.

Minimal damage.

The floor shook, though, and everything happened so fast.

Gregor lost his balance.

Grabbed for the rail.

Missed — his knuckle crashing painfully into a corner.

Then his feet were out from under him, and he felt the room go upside down. His temple cracked against the same corner that had claimed his knuckle. Pain like a hammer blow sliced through him.

Then everything went dark.

Chapter 30

U3 Starship *Defender:* Mercury orbit
Local Date: Undefined
Local Time: Undefined

Jess Mikayla saw the vice director fall. She heard the thick sound his temple made as it struck the rail. Felt the blow as his frail body fell to the floor. She was the first one to his side, removing her jacket and pressing it in a wad against his temple, trying to staunch the pool of blood that flowed freely from an open wound.

"Are you okay, Vice Director?" she said.

But it was obvious he was not okay.

Gregor Anderson's eyes glazed over.

His mouth worked and formed something incoherent.

She knew charter.

She had lost one parent in the UG attack of Atropos and seen the other mangled.

She had seen service during Universe Three's Solar System operations, each designed to slow the Uglies' progress by taking out critical manufacturing and science facilities. With Captain Shudar left behind in the 37 Gem system and with Gregor Anderson's accident, responsibility for this exercise fell to her.

"Get the vice director to the medical bay," she said, striding across the floor and pushing the first security officer she found toward Anderson's crumpled body.

The officer collected himself, then got to work.

She turned to Mazzie Johns, *Defender*'s weapons commander and one of her best friends. "Don't let me down, Mazzie," she said. "Keep the guns blazing — cannons first, fighters second, but I also want someone on developing target coordinates for their main drive. They can't jump now, but they can move."

"Got it, Commander," Mazzie said.

The clean edge of the word *Commander* on Mazzie's lips was something Jess loved about her — Mazzie Johns was one of the smartest people she'd ever met as well as the most grounded, who had no real sense of ego, and so could toggle between personal and professional in a moment's notice.

Anderson had been right to get a S&R event ready, too.

She'd get that working next.

Behind Jess, the security detail was lifting Anderson to a gurney pulled from the emergency storage closet. In the tangled mess of activity, Jess caught the image of the old man's forehead massed up with crimson blood.

"Call ahead to the medics, Stephen," she said to the communications officer. "Let them know the vice director's status and that he's on the way."

Finished with the necessities, Jess came to the bridge's central platform — a location she'd seen Captain Shudar take hundreds of times.

"All right, people," she said as if talking to herself. "Let's see this thing through."

Chapter 31

XB fighter, Mercury orbit
Local Date: Undefined
Local Time: Undefined

The planet flashed into view, then the dark velvet starscape.

Then the sun and the planet, and ... the XB was rolling and tumbling, flashing a strobe of light that dazzled Deidra as she wrestled with the controls.

They were dead, though, those controls. Dead as rocks.

The motion threw her side to side against her straps. She braced herself to hold it together, then locked her gaze to the panel until she got control of herself.

As best she could tell, the ship was spiraling on a path headed directly to Mercury's surface — which flashed into view again, this time so close Deidra thought she could see new craters.

Impact wouldn't be long.

She fired a trim booster — one of only two that still worked.

That helped stabilize them a touch. That was good. At least it calmed the dizzying sensation of the planet flashing by so often. What it didn't do was change the fact that Mercury's surface — pockmarked brown and orange, and already scarred with craters as old as the planet itself — was going to receive another crater.

Ironic, she thought.

After growing up on Mars, and studying so much of the Solar

System itself, Deidra realized she knew almost nothing about Mercury. Only that it was barren and dead, and that it was named for an old god from an old mythology.

Yet, this is where she was going to end up.

In a weird way, she felt relieved.

Her fight was over. She was going out as her father went out — killed by the United Government. At least she got to disable a Star Drive. And they'd succeeded — the triangulation pods had been set.

She toggled the ship's radio. At least that still worked.

"Catazara will be able to set the gate, right?" she said to Feder.

"He will."

"Well, there's that."

"Are we going to be able to land this thing?" Feder asked.

"I don't think so," she called back. "And even if we can, we'll bake as soon as our environmental controller runs out of power."

She gave a cold laugh.

I guess I do know something about Mercury, she thought. It's going to be hot as Hell on the sun side.

"I'm sorry, Allie," she said. "This is the end."

"What about the trims?" Allie replied.

"Not enough juice to change our trajectory."

"Could they slow us down?"

"Not much."

Deidra couldn't bring herself to add that it wouldn't be enough to matter — that they were traveling too fast, that unless Mercury had some kind of atmosphere that she could use as a pressure plate to slow their descent, the trim boosters couldn't change things enough to keep them from being crushed on impact.

The other thing she knew about Mercury was that it had about as much of an atmosphere as the moon —effectively none.

"You've got to try, Deidra," Allie said. "You've got to try something."

"You don't give up, do you?"

"And you do?"

Apparently, yeah, she almost said. The words stuck in her throat, though.

No.

She didn't give up. That had never been her way, and it wasn't going to be now.

I'll do anything to protect my people.

Katriana's words rolled through her head, and she thought about brilliant young Allie Feder sitting behind her.

That's when she saw the display.

Really saw it.

Noted where *Vengeance* was marked as a clouded array of signals, and where *Hercules* still showed as a ship — but more importantly noted a third signal.

The call signals nearly made her cry aloud.

Defender!

They'd been in such a harried state of activity that she'd missed *Defender*'s arrival on the scene, but suddenly *Hercules*'s damaged cannon made sense. It wasn't *Vengeance*'s doing. It was *Defender*.

She couldn't imagine getting out of this derelict XB in one piece, but if she did, she was going to kiss Captain Shudar.

"What is that?" Feder said, obviously seeing the same thing.

"It's *Defender*," Deidra said. "I'm going to get us slowed down. You get on the radio and call Mayday."

She activated both the remaining trim pods, directing them hard-down, toward the rocky surface that loomed so close now she thought she could touch it.

From the backseat she heard Feder's voice.

"*Defender*, this is Allie Feder. I have Director Francis with me. We are on path to crash on Mercury — like really soon now. Any help you might be able to get us would be great."

As Feder spoke, Deidra hit the XB with a full throttle burn that lasted ten seconds before their fuel ran out.

It cut their descent speed by half, which Deidra hoped would now do more than give them both just that much longer to stare out into the darkness of space — which was quite beautiful as she took it in. For a moment she flashed on a time on the Martian surface, standing with her father as he told her the story of Perigee and the origins of Universe Three.

She'd tried to make that vision happen.

Really, she had.

She'd tried to make Universe Three the community Ellyn Parker had first envisioned, a world independent of the frustrations that came under a government of corporations that pretended to be democratic.

She'd tried.
She'd done her best.
Outside, the surface of Mercury drew nearer.

CHAPTER 32

U3 Starship *Defender*: Mercury orbit
Local Date: Undefined
Local Time: Undefined

"Commander?"

Jess started.

It was sensor command.

She turned from the view screen with no little exasperation. With its flurry of activity, the holoprojection system was growing hard to watch. But the observation port let her see what she needed most — *Hercules* was severely damaged, and now *Defender*'s cannons were aiding their fighters to clean UG presence from the entire sector.

The battle was theirs if they could keep pressing.

The rescue operation was working, too, though they would get no more than a pass or two.

"What?" she said to the woman behind the desk.

"It's Signal Intelligence," the woman reported. "They've got an errant U3 spacecraft assigned to *Vengeance* on their system."

She frowned. "Errant?"

"It's damaged, Commander. Freefalling on a course to the planet. Sig Int says they think it's Director Francis."

The room seemed to come to an immediate halt.

"Director Francis?" Jess repeated.

"Yes, Commander. And Professor Feder."

"Is the message real?"

"Vocal patterns match. No reason to think it's not."

"Time to impact?" Jess said, her thoughts falling into place. An XB on full power could get there rapidly, but it had no ability to take on survivors — and that's assuming the director was equipped to survive exposure to space.

"Three minutes, tops."

Three minutes was almost impossible, and any effort would impact other resources.

Still, it was the director.

Maybe.

She gritted her teeth and remembered a debrief with Captain Shudar after one particularly bad mission that had gone sidewise fast. She remembered the relaxed gaze on his face when she asked him how he'd made a split-second decision that had saved the ship, how he'd reached over and patted her hand when she'd asked — in the way that a father might have as he answered it.

When in doubt, he said, *do the right thing*.

"Flight Commander," she said firmly. "Divert the two closest fighters to Mercury on intercept and recon. Explain the damaged ship carries the director and that they are to take whatever steps possible to save her."

Flight conveyed the order.

"Prepare a full transport shuttle, too."

"The transport will be unarmed, Commander."

"Understood. But if by some miracle they can get something done, I want to be ready to collect the director."

Jess's gaze went to the holoprojection.

Defender's weapons were now thinning the nearby space of the UG fighters.

It was even more clear that, barring the arrival of another UG Excelsior ship, the battle itself would be won. There was still work to do, though. Still moving parts to deal with.

The surface of Mercury loomed like a ghost on the observation screen.

She didn't know whether to hope the distress call was really from Director Francis or not.

If it was fake, then maybe the recovery efforts would still find

the director.
    If it was real....
    She shuddered.

Chapter 33

XB fighter, Mercury orbit
Local Date: Undefined
Local Time: Undefined

"Vengeance fighter K-7B, this is Alpha Flight Leader Maxwell Davies flying off Defender, *we have you on-screen."*

The voice startled her.

Deidra Francis toggled the radio.

"Defender squadron?" she replied.

"That's confirmed. Good to hear your voice, Director."

A moment later, with the surface of Mercury suddenly seeming to loom so much closer, Deidra nearly shrieked with joy as a pair of XB spacecraft edged into view, one on each side of theirs.

"Sit tight and let me and Monkey Girl over there have the airwaves a bit, all right?"

"Sitting tight," she said.

Behind her, she could hear Allie Feder crying.

Chapter 34

XB fighter, Mercury orbit
Local Date: Undefined
Local Time: Undefined

Fighting every part of him that wanted to pull up from their dive toward the surface of Mercury, Maxwell "Old Man" Davies toggled the radio. His wing, Charli "Monkey Girl" Conroy, had deployed to the opposite side of the derelict fighter.

The maneuver would be dicey at the best of times, and this was anything but the best of times.

The dead XB was still rotating as it fell — albeit slowly.

He glanced to get visual confirmation of Monkey's position and couldn't help but see that the pilot of the dead craft was, indeed, Deidra Francis, Director of Universe Three. That information did nothing to reduce his stress.

"Are you stable, Monkey?"

"Affirmative."

"Edge up to ten degrees, then close."

"Pincher sling, LC?"

"Affirmative. Once we've latched, full thrusters at one-eighty."

The pair had reduced speed to tuck in beside the director's XB, but now needed to add speed. Ignoring the looming planet surface, he touched the throttle lightly. *Careful,* he thought. The fighter was responsive before it was precise. Such close-in flying took control

— control he wasn't certain Monkey Girl had.

He was happy to hear his wing jump to the conclusion of the pincher, though.

The maneuver would be tricky. Pull ahead, make contact so that the dead XB wouldn't crush theirs when they threw their engines into reverse, and then brake like hell.

Yes, tricky.

And dangerous.

More theoretical than practical, too.

They'd studied the idea based on reports one of their Universe Three undercover agents had stolen from the UG — one where a pair of UG pilots had improvised creating an external sling to catch and save a transport. It had been daring. A maneuver everyone in flight school wanted to go out and practice, but one that was banned for safety purposes. *We can't afford to lose pilots now*, the flight instructor had said. *So, stick with the simulators. Anyone found jacking around will be expelled.*

Then the instructors proved they meant it when, three weeks later, they cut two of the class's better fliers for their joyride.

He hadn't thought about the maneuver since, but as soon as the details of their diversion was outlined, Monkey had called it just as the idea struck him. That made him happy. They'd flown together long enough that they were starting to finish each other's sentences — but just starting. Now, though, Davies wished they'd been able to practice it at least once. A simulator could model the physics of any situation, but it couldn't model the sensation of a real planet looming a very short distance from impact.

The two fighters found their slots, ten degrees ahead of the dead bird. He fought the need to glance at Mercury's surface.

"Close up," Davies said calmly.

He brought his fighter closer. A moment later the edge of his wing laid against that of Director Francis's XB. They were close enough now that the wide whiteness of her eyes froze as a frame in his memory.

On the other side, Monkey Girl did the same.

"Set?" he asked.

"One moment," Monkey said, voice strained.

Davies took that moment to glance at Mercury. They needed stabilization on both sides, or this wasn't going to work. What did they have, twenty seconds? Fifteen?

"Set," Monkey said.

"Bring thrusters to full on three."

He paused for a moment during which he could not feel anything but the sense of time flowing past.

"One ... two ... three."

He pushed reverse thrusters on full back.

Beside him, Monkey Girl did the same.

The engines howled through the fuselage as he pressed the thrusters even harder. The screech of metal on metal was bitter, and for a moment he thought the director's XB was going to slide away. It stuck, though.

The pull of intense g-force bit into his shoulders as the connected spacecraft decelerated together.

Slowly.

Too slowly, Davies was sure.

The brown-orange surface of the planet was close enough now that he could make out ridges that were only a meter tall. He pressed the throttle harder, though it was already at full bore.

The spaceships continued to decelerate.

The rockets of their boosters kicked up a cloud of debris.

Then it was as if everything stopped in place.

And, engines still screaming, the landscape moved away, upward in reverse, lifting.

The scene telescoped out from the planet, and Davies managed to take his gaze off that surface for a moment to see dark space growing in the periphery of his vision.

"*Whoooooooooooooooo!*" It was Monkey.

No time for that, Davies checked his system.

There was no pursuit from *Hercules* fighters, and that was good news.

"Steady thrusters," he called to Monkey. "Let's conserve a bit of fuel for the ride home as we give the director a little bit better view of the planet, shall we?"

"Affirmative, Old Man. A-one-hellacious-firmative."

Davies smiled at her use of his call name.

He was a kid, really — only twenty-three — the youngest of his flight class, which is how he got that call name to begin with. But another mission like this would go a long way toward turning his hair white.

He toggled the radio again.

"*Defender, this is Alpha Flight Leader Davies. I report we have caught the falling rock. Repeat falling rock captured. Request backup.*"

"*Already on the way, Flight Leader. Congratulations on your catch.*"

Davies focused on keeping the throttle steady to ensure he didn't lose contact.

A moment later, his sensor field picked up the signal of the transport that would take Director Francis off his hands.

Chapter 35

U3 Starship *Defender*: Mercury orbit
Local Date: Undefined
Local Time: Undefined

It was painful to have to sit still on the XB while the rescue operation continued around her, but there was little else Deidra Francis could do. Knowing everything else going on around them was so hectic made that anxiety worse.

She wanted to know what was going on but didn't want to interrupt people who were doing critical jobs. She compromised by leaving her radio on broad frequency scan and listening to progress as it occurred. It was, she decided, a beautiful thing, listening to a collection of people working so tightly together, each drawn to the same purpose, each wanting to save the other — or at least it would have been beautiful if the stakes were not so real.

That's how she would remember the event later, she was sure.

At present though, it felt closer to terrifying than pleasurable.

Bursts came to her in snippets of information that she pieced together into stories.

The transport collected the wreckage of her spacecraft, and then sometime later arrived at *Defender*'s loading bay. Once safely in the recovery bay, Deidra extracted herself from the XB fighter, taking a moment to marvel at the damage the little craft had sustained — holes torn through wings, troughs gouged in its fuselage, charred streaks of plasma fire that snaked from nose to tail.

She put her hand on the fuselage and couldn't help but give it a rub.

Behind her, Allie Feder climbed from her seat, Feder cradling her arm as a tech helped her down.

"Are you okay, Allie?" she called back.

"Good as I can be."

"How's the shoulder?"

"Still attached. Probably lost my curveball, but I'll live to integrate again."

Deidra laughed then, and suddenly felt better. She'd saved Allie Feder — or better put, with the random chance that comes from everyone working together, they'd all saved Allie Feder.

"That's good," she said, then continued to listen in on the radio.

As she made her way to the bridge, Deidra knew this much: *Defender*, guided not by Captain Shudar but instead by his second, had come to *Vengeance*'s aid. Gregor had been involved in a fashion she didn't understand, yet — news that surprised her but shouldn't have. *Vengeance* was lost, but rescue operations were underway and there were at least a few survivors.

The ship had disabled *Hercules*. The UG ship was still fundamentally operational, so it would certainly have communicated to their Central Command, and that meant reinforcements were on the way.

The door slid open, and Deidra strode in.

"Welcome aboard *Defender*, Director," Jess Mikayla said.

"Thank you, Jess," she replied. "But where is Captain Shudar?"

"On Apogee," the commander replied. "I thought he was attending your staff session."

"I see," she said, though in truth she did not fully understand. It made sense that her staff would meet in her absence, but not why Mikayla would take the ship. "Did Captain Shudar transfer power to you?"

"Vice Director Anderson commanded the ship here," Mikayla said.

Then the whole thing fell into place.

"That was daring of the vice director." She scanned the bridge and noticed his hover chair empty and pushed to the wall, his cane laid across one brace. She saw also the markings of blood on the floor.

"Where is Gregor now? Is he well?"

"In the medical center, Director. He fell and hit his head. I've been too busy to follow up, but the medics were informed quickly."

Deidra grimaced.

"What is your ship's status otherwise?"

"Our internals are positive, Director. No damage of merit. We've lost four fighters in the defense. *Vengeance*, too, but rescue operations are in action. We have survivors on board. Time is short, though. I intend this to be our last pass."

"Is there anything you need?"

"A couple extra Star Drives to defend the perimeter."

Deidra gave a grim nod. "No such luck," she said.

"Well, then, I'd say we're fully deployed and operational."

Deidra turned her gaze to the display, taking in the scintillating cloud of the signal that would otherwise be Captain Keyes's spacecraft. She wondered if Keyes would be among the survivors.

"Director?" Mikayla said.

Deidra turned her gaze back to the officer's.

"The UG ship is derelict. Engines dead. Guns dead. Only a few straggling fighters being collected as we speak."

"Yes?"

"Should I order the ship destroyed?"

The question hung there like a bomb itself.

The *Hercules* was a major asset for the United Government hence its destruction would be a boon. It was a military target. It had killed *Vengeance*. The spacecraft was fair game.

But it was also defenseless now.

To kill *Hercules* would be an execution no different from its action against *Vengeance*.

Deidra's gaze flashed to the floor where Gregor Anderson's bloodstain was still visible.

It made her think of her father. What would Casmir Francis, leader of Universe Three, have done here? How about Perigee?

It was the smart move to put *Hercules* down, though — the decision that would provide the most safety for her Universe Three compatriots.

Commander Mikayla was still young. The idiosyncrasies of life had thrown her into the deepest of space in this most difficult of moment's. Her training had served her well in battle operations, and it told her what she needed to do now, but Deidra wasn't sure Mikayla had the heart to be at the helm for such a command.

Deidra didn't want to destroy her by forcing her to make that call.

"Collect our people," Deidra said. "That's our first purpose."

"All right."

Deidra wasn't sure the commander's expression was one of disappointment or relief.

Both, probably.

It was an odd mix of emotions that matched her own.

"Carry that out, then get us the hell out of here," she said to the commander. "I'm going to the medical bay to see how the vice director is getting along."

Chapter 36

U3 Starship *Defender*: Mercury orbit
Local Date: Undefined
Local Time: Undefined

Lying in sick bay, Gregor looked horrible.

A helmet of thick white gauze crowned his head, but a dark burgundy bruise had flowed down the side of his face to pool finally around his chin. The folds around that side of his neck were likewise darkened. The rest of his skin was lined and pasty, and the blue tones of the room's lighting paired with readouts from a bank of machines he'd been attached to, adding a coldness to his aura.

His eyes were closed, his arms lay flaccid at each side.

At random moments, thin groans of pain escaped Gregor Anderson's lips.

"How is he?" Deidra asked the doctor as a medic bot worked to change a fluid bag that was dripping into Gregor's IV.

An antiseptic sting made her want to wrinkle her nose.

"He's had bleeding into his brain," the doctor replied. "He's also broken his hip and cracked his patella. Assuming he recovers I doubt he'll ever walk again without full augmentation. But it's the brain bleed that's the real problem. We have shunts in place, but damage has already been done. We have him sedated. Working to keep his swelling down. If we can keep that from getting too bad, we can start stem cell conversion. Until then we don't want to do more harm than good."

"Do you expect him to make it?"

"I can't say, Director. The body is the miraculous thing, and I hear he fights like a tiger."

She wanted to take encouragement from the doctor's words, but as he spoke, the medic's expression told a different story from behind him. Gregor was in trouble. The doctor did not expect him to make it through.

"You hear right," Deidra said. "He does indeed fight like a tiger. Thank you."

Deidra reached down to take Gregor's hand.

It was cool and thin, delicate to her touch. When she pressed her palm to his, she felt the pressure of his grip tighten in response.

"Gregor?"

The eye on the unmarred side of the old man's face flickered open. His chest rose with a deeper breath.

"Deidra. You're alive."

"Only because you came and got me."

Gregor's smile was a painful pulling back of his lips against his teeth. "It's what your father would have done."

"He'd be proud of you, Gregor." She gripped his hand as tightly as she felt comfortable doing. He was frail now. So frail. She remembered him otherwise, though, standing with her father, both younger and vigorous, with hair dark and smiles that flashed wide. "You know that, right? Papa loved you like a brother. We'd be nowhere without you."

He tried to shrug then groaned in pain.

"The gate," Gregor said with a raspy breath.

"It's set, Gregor. The mission was success."

This time his smile was a calmly satisfied curling of the unbruised side of his face.

"Is good,' he whispered.

His hand gave a single firm grip, then fell limp.

One of the machines blipped loudly. Another gave a low whine.

Deidra stepped away as the doctor and three nurses sprang to action. She watched them work for a moment, but knew it was not going to help. Gregor Anderson was gone.

"Godspeed, my friend," she said.

As she left sickbay, a tear seeped from the corner of her eye, and she felt the heavy turning of a page of history.

The first generation had now passed.

Now they were alone, she thought, as she walked toward the bridge. Now the experiment that was Universe Three would be put to the ultimate test.

She needed to be strong.

Her stride gained momentum with each step. She stood stronger, then, feeling a resolute sense of purpose the seemed to glow inside her entire being.

She would do what needed to be done.

Chapter 37

U3 Starship *Defender*: Mercury orbit
Local Date: Undefined
Local Time: Undefined

This time, Deidra Francis entered the bridge at a stiff pace, strands of her hair flying from her face as she strode to the center of the command platform.

"I declare command of this ship from this point until I relinquish it," she said, her voice firm and crisp.

She felt Commander Mikayla's gaze at the periphery of her vision, so turned to her.

"You've done well, Jess. If we get home safely you will have my commendation, as well as my thanks."

The commander's body language showed tension then. She pressed her hands together as if in conflict with each other, the set of her jaw tightened, and yet the muscles around her eyes relaxed as if she was relieved, as if she understood everything that was going to happen.

"I acknowledge the director," Mikayla called back.

If there was a hesitation throughout the room, it was brief.

"Weapons Command," Deidra called. "Prepare cannons,"

"Cannons prepared, Director."

"Fire on *Hercules* at will."

"Direct hit with both cannons, Director."

"Again," Deidra said calmly.

"Two more direct hits, Director."

"Again."

Deidra turned to the commander. "What is the status of our recovery missions?"

"Nearly complete," Mikayla replied.

"Continue to monitor progress. Report to me when the last ship has been collected."

"Understood."

Deidra returned her gaze to the weapons command.

"Again."

She watched the display in the center of the bridge's airspace as *Defender* carved *Hercules* into pieces, just as *Hercules* had done to *Vengeance* earlier.

Small indicators of *Defender*'s rescue shuttles drew closer.

A timer ran in one part of the display.

How long before the United Government's next arrival would come?

It took time to prepare star jump, but there *would* be more arrivals. And it was true that Universe Three could not afford to lose another Excelsior class battle cruiser.

Her mind flashed to the time long ago when Universe Three had bugged out of Mars colony. She remembered how her father had stayed on the ground until the end, refusing to board the final shuttle before all other members of the community had been gathered.

She thought of Gregor, the last of her father's compatriots, now dead.

She would not leave her people here to die.

She had seen a similar tone to Commander Mikayla's performance — something she would remember when the time was right. It was clear Mikayla was both bright and decisive. Traits that would serve her well as she matured. It was clear Mikayla had wanted to make this call and was already planning to do so when she first raised the question to Deidra.

She was young, though.

Young to make such coldhearted calculations.

"Again," she called.

Defender's cannons flared again.

And again.

And again.

"The final rescue shuttle has entered the loading bay, Director," Commander Mikayla said.

Deidra stood straight then, releasing her hold on the rail that she realized only now had been so firm her hands were white.

She took a breath deep enough that it made her ribs ache.

"Commander Mikayla," she said. "I give control of *Defender* back to your hands. Get us the hell out of here."

"Thank you, Director," Mikayla replied. "All stations prepare for jump."

Less than a minute later, Commander Jessamin Mikayla began her checklist routine with each station. When she got to the end, she took one last glance at the projection that showed only *Defender* and two ghostlike clouds of debris.

"Commence jump," she said with a dry tone. "Enjoy the show."

HISTORY

What would later be known as the Battle of Mercury was over almost before it began.

A barrage of plasma fire fell from Defender*'s guns, destroying* Hercules*'s cannons with devastating accuracy. The fighters of both* Excelsior *spacecraft (and eventually their shuttles and skimmers and anything with guns) engaged in the most complex episode of space battle the human universe had ever seen. Dogfights in deep space played out amid scattered remains of spacecraft, leaving pilots to dodge both plasma fire and a most modern form of flak.*

The ending was preordained, though, by the disabling of Hercules*'s cannons.*

With no method to defend themselves from Defender*'s long-range weapons, and no ability to jump, the United Government's battle cruiser was as doomed as* Vengeance *had been before.*

In less than thirty minutes, Hercules *local ion drive engines were also put out of commission, and the end was clear.*

Hercules*'s only hope was the arrival of another UGIS Star Drive ship — an effort that, as the fates of war would have it, was delayed for several hours when UG military leaders thought distress calls from* Hercules *were a U3 ruse intended to draw their resources from other important missions.*

When finally launched, the reinforcement mission arrived far too late.

HOMEFRONT

CHAPTER 38

Crystal City, Virginia
Local Date: July 3, 2252
Local Time: 1915

When Zina Nichols stepped off the J-Line red car and into Washington Station, she was so tired she thought she might fall off her feet. She had never been able to sleep while traveling, which meant that the last time she'd gotten out of bed was yesterday morning two days ago. The station was hot and sticky with the usual compression of human bodies and the unusually heavy midsummer humidity of the city — which she felt as a bitter taste at the back of her tongue.

She checked her clock as she pushed through a throng of workers.

7:18 PM.

Her last meal was a rice and gravy composite she'd shoved down her throat before the shuttle launched, and her stomach was burning something between being entirely empty and being full of acid. Her whole body felt both dead and restless at the same time.

She most desperately needed a dinner, a sleep, and a workout.

In that order.

A shower wouldn't hurt, either.

Add to it the fact that reentry had been rockier than normal, and that the transport car had been rush hour crowded, and you had one UGIO primary investigator who was not in her best of moods.

At least the taxi pod was a one-holer, which meant it had been quiet enough she could hear her own thoughts.

She would have fallen asleep if she could have.

Alas, that was not her style either.

The sessions had gone well. She had already passed notes to Willim Pinot. Thomas Kitchell understood the score. She was as certain as she could be that he would play his part in making the Torrance Black thing go away. She played scenarios through her mind as the taxi pod made its way through streets clogged with traffic.

Hover drives that could adjust altitude couldn't come fast enough for her.

A forty-five-minute ride later, the pod dropped her off in front of a red brick apartment building that was now darkening to deep, midnight maroon as the sun fell further below the horizon.

She liked the building.

The place felt strong. Stable. Maybe it was just her imagination, but it felt even bigger this evening as she stood before it, breathing in the smells of shrubbery planted in garden holes built into the concrete paths. She smelled rain on the air that made her happy somehow. That the building had been constructed three centuries ago gave it a sense of permanence, and zoning laws kept the area quiet.

The apartment itself was small. Just the living area, a kitchen, a bathroom, and the bedroom, but they didn't spend much time here, so it served their purposes.

She hoped Zi-Chau would be working late this evening.

Unfortunately, that was not the case.

"You're home," he called in his most grandiose "host with the most" voice as she entered their apartment.

He was in the kitchen.

The aroma and sound of onions and peppers sizzling in a skillet made her forget her regret that he was home.

She nearly swooned with hunger.

"And so are you," she replied.

She shouldered her travel bag onto the couch, then went to the kitchen to find Zi-Chau, her lover of the past two years, standing with arms outstretched — one hand holding a stainless stirring spoon — and creases in his dark face deepening as he smiled for her.

Even discounting her own slightness, he was a tall man — lithe when he was younger but now sporting a small pouch along his belly and sides that foretold of more to come. Love handles, she'd tell him when he worried over it. He still wore his work pants, but only a wrinkled undergarment as a shirt. He'd removed his polished shoes and wore his indoor sandals instead.

"Just got home," he said as she stepped into his hug.

She laid her head onto his chest — as much to use him as a prop to keep on her feet as to return his sentiment. She wrapped her arms around him, though, leaning into him and letting her fingers press gently onto his shoulders. Zi-Chau was a good man, even if sometimes unable to read the moment.

"Are you all right?" Zi-Chau asked.

Zina took in the counter where Zi-Chau had piled chopped onions, peppers, pasta, and grated feta sorted into a production line of sorts. Delicate decanters of oil sat opposite the skillet.

She eyed him wearily.

Comfort food.

It was a meal he made most often when he was under stress at the chief of staff's office.

"I'm hungry and tired," she said. "Are you all right?"

He gave a stunted laugh. "Yes," he said. "I am fine also."

But she knew better. She had learned shortly after they had met how to interpret most everything he did. He was hiding something — or she supposed that he might have something on his mind that he simply didn't want to talk about. The idea of not talking appealed to her, but his reluctance to share perked up her ears.

"You take this one," he said, sliding the peppers and onions that had been on the skillet onto the plate of pasta. "I'll make myself some more."

Her stomach wasn't going to argue with that.

She took the plate and went to the dinner table, then dug in.

"Delicious," she said.

"Nothing but the finest for my sweetie."

"Be careful or you'll have me fat and slothful before you know it," she said after another bite.

"Then I will just kick you to the side of the road," he joked, his laughter this time more robust.

It was a routine conversation for them both.

Zi-Chau Holloway was twenty years her senior, and as an adjutant to Admiral Henni Gould, the chief of staff to the UG security council, he had a degree of power. When Zina had first attached herself to him, people were quick to jump to the idea that she was simply a trophy, a young, attractive enough nobody buried in the bureaucracy someplace so deep no one could find room to care about, somebody that he would dally with, and eventually *kick to the side of the road*, as one of his drunken compatriots had so inappropriately said out loud at a party one evening a few weeks after they'd moved in together.

It would have angered her if it had not been true.

It would also have angered her if the opposite were not also true. Zi-Chau Holloway *was* most certainly a good man, good enough anyway, but she had no intention of making a life with him.

The idea of any true pairing held no interest for her.

Though Zi-Chau would never have said it aloud, she saw through his demeanor well enough to know this was also true for him.

Perhaps he would change as he grew from an older man to a truly old man.

Perhaps then he would want something deeper — or at least something more dependable.

But for now, their relationship fit the profile. He enjoyed being seen with young women simply for the vibe it gave off. In return, he helped them. So, it was true that Zi-Chau treated her kindly, but also as a young puppy of sorts.

Which was fine by her.

It was all her advantage in the end.

She let him explain how the agency worked, and then cross-indexed his commentary with other sources of information to arrive at a profile on what things she could believe from him, and what others she could not.

He was, for example, open with fleet deployments when it came to science missions, but less so with missions focused on sorting out the location of Universe Three outposts. He would not give direct information about U3 spies in the system, but she could, it turned out, coax him into dropping enough information about them that she could again cross-index other reports to find them on her own.

In the earliest days she thought he was aware that she was using him as much as he was using her. But as the weeks passed, Zina came to understand he was more simple than she'd first thought. He considered himself astute, but mostly he was oblivious to things he didn't think of as threats.

Today, for example, as she ate the pasta, she noted his datapad crooked up at an angle against the kitchen counter backsplash so he could keep up with a conversation as he worked, its projection screen set in a way that said he thought she couldn't see it.

But she could, indeed, see it.

At least well enough that, as the sizzle of another serving of peppers hitting the skillet filled the room, and as Zi-Chau split his attention between the skillet and the display, she could make out the basics.

She adjusted an app in her dataclip to add a touch of zoom and precision.

Something was going on.

Some kind of skirmish.

Mercury? The planet?

Yes, Mercury.

And *Hercules*.

Both words kept coming up. *Initial reports indicate positive progress.*

He grunted under his breath, stirring the mixture, then used his free hand to signal a comment into the conversation.

Zina ate more of her dinner and did her best to avoid being seen eavesdropping.

"Are you sure everything is okay?" she said.

"Of course they are."

"You just seem distracted."

"It's … it's just … well, you know how it is."

"Yes, honey," she said. "You just can't talk about it."

"That's what I love about you," Zi-Chau replied. "Always so understanding."

"I work with secrets, too," she said.

"Yes, you do.," He nodded as he poured his own plate of pasta, smiling the over-big smile he always got when he was dismissing her.

She ate more pasta.

"This is really delicious," she said. "Thank you. I didn't realize how hungry I was."

He shut down his display, then carried his own plate to sit with her.

She smiled.

Patience, she thought.

Zi-Chau was fatigued. And he'd been drinking. He would eat his dinner and on normal days they would watch something together, but tonight he would go to bed early — most likely with a comment about needing to go in early tomorrow to deal with whatever was happening around Mercury.

Zina set an alarm for herself, realizing she wasn't going to get as much sleep as she wanted, but that it would be worth it in the end.

"I'm completely bushed," she said, taking her plate to the cleaner. "I don't think I've slept in two days, so I'm going to go ahead to bed."

"I'm sure that would be for the best," Zi-Chau said.

She kissed the top of his head as she left, noting that he reengaged his display as she left the kitchen and went to the bedroom.

Her alarm would wake her soon.

Then she would break into Zi-Chau's datapad and find out what was going on.

Chapter 39

Science Station Tiger-3, Mars Colony Kasbian
Local Date: July 4, 2252 (Earth Standard)
Local Time: 1505

Thomas Kitchell glanced at the clock of his dataclip for the fourth time in the last minute.

Ragnath Gavarian was now officially late, and Kitchell was as nervous as he could ever remember being. It was two days since LUMI had officially cancelled his talk, meaning one day since he'd hopped a jump shuttle and made it back "home" to Tiger-3, a domed environment that included the entire population of the colony.

The new jump shuttles were great — smaller versions of the huge engines that drove Excelsior-class ships, designed to make intrasolar travel as fast and uneventful for smaller craft as interstellar was for Star Drives. *Venus for breakfast, Neptune for dinner*, as the advertisements went. They cut travel time from Mars to Luna from months down to simply the few hours it took to get to and from the stations themselves.

It was a helluva lot easier than traveling on the simple thrust, star sail, or impulse/ion drive engines that poked along at a fraction of light speed.

Unfortunately, he knew those connections were siphoning Alpha Centauri A.

Sure, the energy drain that a jump shuttle took was small compared to Excelsior drives, but there could be thousands of them, and $E=Mc^2$.

Always had, always would.

Run out of "M" then no more "E."

Maybe it would be better if he wasn't so sensitive to the latest reports that said power out of Alpha Centauri A had been steadily waning. The last runs of the models said that the wormhole reservoir of the star would last fifty more years before the multidimensional friction associated with the gate would make extracting the star's energy too difficult to sustain travel.

Kitchell knew it would be worse than that.

Sooner than everyone thought, anyway, especially after the UG let these small transportation companies tap into the energy stream. It wouldn't stop there. Every business in the system was lobbying for their little sliver of the star pie.

He tried not to think about it, though — tried not to get too angry when UG leadership chartered a series of projects to decide which star would be the next target when this one ran out of juice.

Today it was easier to ignore the situation, though, because today everything was going to hell for Kitchell personally.

He'd spent the last half hour literally pacing through the cluttered but private little apartment he'd been assigned back in the days when his only concern was what to do next on an advanced ion-radio processing system that the UG had asked him to work on. The apartment was comfortable enough, but floorspace was at a premium, meaning he continually sidestepped the stacks of equipment he'd shoved against the wall or left hanging out over the edges of small tables — mostly receivers and component boards he was using to fiddle with low-frequency quantum particles.

He had no idea what to do about Investigator Nichols, but the pressure was getting to him.

His head hurt.

His lungs ached.

His legs felt like they were going to cramp with every step.

True to Nichols's prediction, by the time he made it home, reporters had filled Kitchell's comm system to the brim asking for his story.

He'd chosen to go exclusively with Ragnath Gavarian, partially because his profile was so extensive and his reputation was so certain. Gavarian was the prizewinning and system-renowned investigative journalist whose name had been on the byline of the stories breaking the biggest scandals of the past few years. If anyone was to be believed, Ragnath Gavarian would be the guy. But Kitchell had also chosen him because Gavarian was one of the few reporters who agreed to meet informally where the others had wanted larger sessions with their assistants flittering around, or worse, interviews with formal video shoots.

As if Kitchell wanted to get his mug on the vids now.

The idea made him want to vomit more than a little bit.

The biggest factor in the choice, however, was that Gavarian had chatted with him for hours during his commute home, often spending long chunks of time listening to Kitchell's more esoteric stories, then playing "I can top that."

As they were calling it a night, Kitchell asked the reporter if he did this with all his contacts and was surprised to hear Gavarian say yes.

"I figure that if I want you to trust me, I need to trust you. If you feel comfortable opening up to me, I need to feel comfortable opening up to you."

Before that call was over, Kitchell decided he liked the man.

The only question now was to decide exactly what story Kitchell was going to tell him.

Could he truly hang Torrance Black out to dry?

With each pacing step his mind played different versions of different conversations he might have with Gavarian.

The UGIO had made it clear that his job was to simply avoid supporting Torrance Black.

He didn't have to come out and accuse Torrance of anything at all. Instead, they expected him to simply leave open questions dangling.

"Yes, it is definitely odd that he's gone off the grid so deeply," he was to say when Gavarian pressed him on rumors surrounding Torrance's disappearance. *"I don't understand why he would do that."*

"I suppose anything is possible," he was to reply when asked whether Torrance could have been tied to Universe Three. *"I can't say I saw anything directly, but we all know Torrance had*

connections everywhere, and anyone who is paying attention knows how deep Universe Three tendrils go."

He was supposed to shrug as often as needed.

Supposed to be exasperated — be tortured and torn by his uncertainty but leave the door open for the public's courtroom to make their own decisions.

And he knew the result in advance.

Enough of that public court would make the decision to convict Torrance that the accusation alone would stick. The UG would strip Torrance of rank and position in absentia, people would strip him of everything else.

He believed Investigator Nichols's intense sincerity. If he went against her wishes, things could get ... ugly.

The only thing that made it possible for Kitchell to contemplate these things at all was that his part was about saving Marisa Harthing — and himself, of course. But honestly, he was sure he'd tell them to shove off it if wasn't for Marisa.

If Marisa knew his situation, she'd tell him not to worry about her, but he couldn't help how he felt.

The alternative was to tell Gavarian the truth.

Could he do that?

Goddamn it, he kept muttering to himself.

Memories of the press associated with *Everguard* kept flowing over him. He'd been such a kid then. Quick with a comment. Eminently quotable. A reporter's delight. The attention had been heady and exciting — all the way up until he wanted it all to go away, and it wouldn't.

He'd hated that.

All he wanted to do was to live his life and do his work. It was all he'd ever wanted to do. Now he was stuck in a moment that felt like *Everguard* all over again, but magnitudes worse.

Protect the United Government or protect Torrance Black?

The question made his head explode.

Either way, though, Torrance was going down.

Why?

He kept coming to that question.

Why were the UGIO convinced that Torrance needed to be ruined? He didn't know, but he didn't like the pressure that built whenever he let the question rattle around in his mind. He felt sharks moving in waters he couldn't see.

Where was Torrance?

Could he be dead?

Ambassadors didn't just fall off the face of the universe, after all.

Could he have missed something?

Kitchell could be gullible, or at least oblivious enough to miss certain realities at times. Was it *actually* possible that Torrance Black had been a double agent all the time?

No.

Torrance wasn't like that. There was just no way.

So, no. Absolutely, no.

When the tone to his door finally rang, Thomas Kitchell, so deep into his own thoughts, tripped over a wave generator he'd left out too far.

Chapter 40

Science Station Tiger-3, Mars Colony Kasbian
Local Date: July 4, 2252 (Earth Standard)
Local Time: 1511

Calming himself, Kitchell stood straighter, flexing his toe to ensure he hadn't broken anything. Pain throbbed, but he thought he was probably fine.

"Klaus," he said. "Please open the door."

The door slid open.

"Klaus?" the man standing in the foyer said, having obviously heard him.

Ragnath Gavarian looked young for his years, trim and fit, wearing dark trousers and a thin jacket that hugged his contours. His thick, dark hair was cut short, and his cheekbones were sharp enough they could cut glass. He had augmented his blue eyes to a crystalline clarity that made it almost impossible to look anywhere else. A silver dataclip wrapped around one ear, its leads running into the canal to attach to implants in his brain.

"Mr. Gavarian," Kitchell said, running his hand sheepishly through his thinning hair and giving an embarrassed grin. "Yeah. I call my system Klaus because it's not Gauss."

"Not Gauss?"

"As in the mathematician, you know. Noise hides what's inside like a door hides what's opposite?"

Gavarian made a patient smile.

"Silly story, I guess."

"Not silly at all."

Kitchell shrugged. "It makes me happy, anyway."

"And who is to question that?"

Realizing that his guest hadn't moved since the door opened, Kitchell hurriedly got out of the way. "Come in," he said. "Come in."

The journalist entered.

"Thanks so much for agreeing to come here," Kitchell said. "I apologize for the mess."

"Not a problem at all, Thomas," Gavarian said. "May I call you Thomas?"

"Of course."

The journalist came fully into the room and took in its full splendor.

"And this *mess* is not a problem either," Gavarian said with a smile. "Believe me when I say I've seen a lot worse. To be honest I kind of like it."

Only then did Kitchell notice he'd left the remains of last night's dinner on a countertop, and only then did he realize exactly how *many* models and prototypes he'd left scattered about the room.

His cheeks flushed with embarrassment, and he picked up the now empty carton of rice curry.

"Well," Kitchell said, depositing the trash into the converter. "I suppose it's more weirdness than mess."

"Weird is wonderful," Gavarian said as he peered into a controller system Kitchell had been fiddling with for weeks now. "Is that a mass-energy monitor?" he said with a tone of glee that made the journalist sound boyish.

"Yeah," Kitchell replied. "The left-hand pane is, anyway. Nice to see someone without a physics degree pick that kind of thing up."

Gavarian stood straight. "Hey, I like weird."

Kitchell gave a nervous laugh, but he now understood why the world regarded Gavarian so highly. Less than a minute in, and Kitchell was already calm and already intrigued enough to want to find out who this journalist really was.

"Would you like something to drink, or do you prefer to just get down to business?"

"A tall glass of tea would be great."

"Iced or warmed?"

"Ice, please. Maybe a dash of something citrus?"

"Will do."

He turned to get the drinks, realizing that his patter was a cover. On one hand, he wanted this interview to be over, but on the other, if it went on forever, he never needed to decide about Torrance.

A moment later he returned with Gavarian's glass and a large cup of steaming coffee for himself.

Gavarian had taken one of the hardbacked chairs Kitchell had pushed up against the far wall a month ago.

The journalist took a sip.

"Outstanding," he said. "Orange, right?"

"Right."

"I'll have to get your model number. Mine is always going too soft on the citrus."

Kitchell put his cup on a side table beside the padded recliner he called his "couch."

"How would you like to get started?" he said.

"Well," Gavarian said, putting his glass on the table, too. "Maybe you could tell me about your time with Torrance Black. I know the basic legend — you were a precocious kid and the ambassador picked you out of a lineup or something like that, right?"

"A lineup. Yeah. That's about right. I can still remember the day LC came to class looking for this asshole kid who sprayed a compartment with tomato paste. I was a bit of a delinquent, I suppose."

"A lovable one, it seems."

"Lovable enough to salvage, anyway." He sipped his coffee again and set the cup down with a soft clink.

Kitchell spoke about their time on *Everguard*, the events of the attack, the killing of Malloy, and then Torrance's involvement in getting him a premium scholarship to pursue his studies.

"I did three degrees in various elements of signal processing," Kitchell said with perhaps too much pride. "The last from LUMI."

Gavarian sipped the last of his tea.

"That's impressive."

The reporter dropped his tone a notch, and Kitchell felt the introductory part of the conversation end as fully as if Klaus the

Door had slammed it shut.

"You know I have to ask about Torrance Black and Universe Three, right?"

"Yeah," Kitchell said, taking a resigned breath. "I know you do."

"Is it true? Was he an agent?"

He looked at Gavarian.

This was the moment.

Tell the truth, or leave the door open for the world to roll over his friend.

He drew a deep breath and stared into the crystalline clarity of Ragnath Gavarian's gaze. From the recesses of his mind, he heard a phrase and felt, more than recalled, the image of Torrance Black in his system command chair, winking at him.

Torrance's voice seemed to come from somewhere inside his veins.

Take a chance, right?

He knew what he had to do.

"No, Ragnath," he said as firmly as his voice would carry. "Torrance Black has never been associated with Universe Three, and anyone who says he was ... is lying through their teeth. But the United Government is doing its best to pretend that he was, and that includes trying to extort me and probably Marisa Harthing to keep us quiet."

The expression on the journalist's face was hard to read, but the shine in his eyes was clear.

The man smelled red meat.

"Okay," he said as he settled back. "Tell me about it."

For the next half hour, Thomas Kitchell did just that.

"You know you're going to have to leave, don't you?" Gavarian said as they were finishing. "This is going to cause some pretty big shockwaves. You're going to have to get out of here, like right now."

Kitchell nodded. "I suppose you're right."

"Do you have anywhere to go?"

"I haven't really thought that far."

"Well, I'd say you've got two days at best. So, you'd better start thinking."

"Only two?"

"At best. It will take a day to build the story, and I can probably put off publication for another twenty-four standard hours. But that's the top end. After that, the clock is ticking — and it'll be a really fast clock."

"I know how that goes."

"And that's only if the UG doesn't already know you're talking."

His gut gave him a kick then. The knife-edged gleam in the investigator's eyes came back to him. Gavarian was right. The UGIO would be watching him.

He had security systems around him, of course.

All the classic stuff, as well as special devices of his own making. But UGIO spies had their own special devices, too, and his clearances only went so far.

It was a definite possibility they had access to his airwaves.

Had they been able to hear what he'd already said?

If so, the clock started now.

He really did need to get off the station fast.

He put his head in his hands.

"I really didn't think this through."

Gavarian leaned in. "I've got people who can help," he said in a low whisper.

"Who?"

The journalist gave a close-lipped grin, then shook his head before gesturing to a datapad on the counter.

The message was clear. He'd contact Kitchell that way.

Kitchell grunted his understanding, feeling a strange sense of relief due simply to being with someone who had a plan — even as limited as that plan might be.

The journalist then took Kitchell by both shoulders and gave him a *hang in there* stare that carried hundreds of words on it. Words like "I've played this game before" and "I've got people who can get you off the grid."

A storm was coming, and the UGIO was not an organization that would play fair.

UG intelligence would use his flight against him, of course, but they were already planning to lock him up forever anyway.

What did he have to lose?

Chapter 41

Crystal City, Virginia
Local Date: July 4, 2252 (Earth Standard)
Local Time: 1142

Her alarm pulsed a soft stream of hazy sound somewhere in the distance. Zina Nichols rolled to her side and pulled a silk sheet over her head, remembering her activity last night as she came awake — recalling stealing into Zi-Chau's message channels somewhere past midnight, thinking about what she'd learned.

Her body felt leaden and slow, but her mind picked up speed.

Universe Three had attacked from behind planet Mercury.

Or, better said, their attack had been thwarted there.

The UG had killed the U3 ship *Vengeance*, but lost *Hercules* in the process. That alone was a good trade-off. A war of attrition favored the UG by a far margin.

What did it mean?

She'd been too tired to think it through last night, but her dream state had been working on it, crossing the information in Zi-Chau's conversations with intel reports she'd seen over the past several months — mission profiles from U3, for example, and data pulled from the all-too-rare bits of communication intercepted during their jumps into the Solar System.

She was sensing things in her gut now that felt important, but that she couldn't quite grasp.

She'd come to rely on that sensation, though.

Something big was happening.

These thoughts all rolled through her tired mind as the buzzer grew sharper.

The buzzer.

She sat bolt upright. It was her communications channel.

Someone waited at the end of the line.

She glanced to Zi-Chau's side of the bed and saw it was long empty. Her data feed said it was nearing noon. He would be at work now, at work and dealing with whatever the fallout was of this thing around Mercury.

"Answer call."

The buzzer cut off. *"Connecting."*

The delay meant the call came from a secure node. She steeled herself.

Kitchell. It had to be about Kitchell.

She'd been certain enough of the scientist to think he'd play his part, but not stupid enough to bank everything she had on it. She'd ordered surveillance on his communications and his apartment and had asked the assistant Pinot had given her to call directly if it produced anything.

The system gave the double click.

"Activated."

"What is it?" she said.

"The scientist is talking," a distorted voice came from the other end.

"And the story he's telling?"

"Not the good one."

Zina sat on the bed, feeling the weight of the crumpled sheets over her folded legs. Air from a ceiling fan was cool against her skin. The dynamic image of the lily on her forearm folded in response to the chill. Her lioness seemed to growl.

Damn it.

She drew a deep breath. The lily came back to its full position, the purple shades glowing again.

"You know the next step."

"Neutralize the asset."

"Yes, please."

"I understand."

She ran her fingers through tangled hair.

"Close call," she said.

The system clicked off, and the only sound was street noise that filtered in from the apartment window.

She grumbled.

She had liked Kitchell.

It pained her to take him down, but his case would be easy. He'd been deeply involved in the code work and technology development they were using to track Universe Three. He was, therefore, positioned perfectly to feed U3 anything they needed to avoid detection — it meant, in fact, that Thomas Kitchell could even make direct interventions into the data to ensure no one could find the terrorists if they got too close. Interventions she could create without detection if she touched on the right contacts. The mere fact that the terrorists had avoided detection for so long could be twisted against him without too much effort.

Kitchell was an independent citizen, not aligned to any organization.

So, the case against him would be simple.

Marisa Harthing, being a ranking officer in the UG Interstellar Command, would be a more inconvenient situation.

Then there was Pinot to manage.

She'd told the director she thought the scientist would hold the line, so he'd need something to keep her in his good graces. It was workable. Perhaps she could mine something more from Zi-Chau's secret conversations.

Perhaps, anyway.

She didn't want to get caught up in false hopes.

She weighed her options as she slid her legs off the bed, then stood up to stretch and relieve the tightness that ran down her back and into her legs.

She had a few hours before Pinot would call her to his office.

She needed a shower. Then breakfast.

There were things she needed to think about.

It was as she was stepping into the shower that she asked herself what turned out to be the right question.

Why would Universe Three launch an operation from behind Mercury?

And it was only after she had stepped out of the shower and was drying her hair that the answer came to her.

CHAPTER 42

Mars Colony Kasbian
Local Date: July 4, 2252 (Earth Standard)
Local Time: 2220

The taxi pod pulled up, floating silently on its antigrav engines. It was a small pod — a single-seater as, since the hours were growing later, Thomas Kitchell had expected it would be. As the taxi came to a stop, he gazed into the darkness, taking in the gauzy sight of the dome above them, thinking about the massive array of technologies that had gone into creating the enclosed environment he'd been living in.

By daylight, the clear dome gave view to the surrounding landscape — orange and dry, stretching out to a ridge of stark Martian mountains. The dome served to capture heat, which the community converted into battery power. At nighttime, however, the inner curve of the dome reflected light from the colony, obfuscating the view and warping it by pasting a human-created mess over the star-pattern of deep space.

The taxi's door gull winged open, and Kitchell stepped in to take a seat.

His stomach gave an acidic double clutch.

What had he gotten into?

Would this be the last time he saw this sight?

"Destination?" the machine said.

"Darsi Research Facility, Building Six," he replied.

The door closed and sealed with a tight whine that accentuated the entire over-the-top essence of "top-secret agent" he'd been feeling since receiving Gavarian's encrypted note, which included a set of coordinates and a time.

It was that time that had given him the metaphorical slap in the face he'd needed to get going.

Three hours.

That's how long he had.

Before he skipped the station, Kitchell needed to grab bits of his work to take with him.

So, he called a taxi pod and, as it guided him to the office, he watched lights of the city slide past and wondered where Gavarian's people were taking him that would be "off the grid."

All he knew for sure was that the plan said he'd stay at least two days at the first contact — then go to a place labeled simply Safe House #3.

What he would do after that was up in the air.

He was guessing that Safe House #3 was someplace in the wilds of the asteroid belt. The belt was the only place in the Solar System where a group of renegades could keep someone fully under wraps.

Would they jump him there? If so, could the UG track the jump?

That was a bit of work he'd been pursuing himself recently, working with Quay Ti-Taan and a collection of other ultra-quick people to see if it was possible to track a Star Drive's destination from the wave particle remnants of their jump process.

From what he could tell, the answer was "probably," but the pieces of work he'd touched suggested the final answer was a few years away. Of course, he wasn't the only one working on the project, and the project's classification meant he didn't know what everyone else was doing. It was at least possible Ti-Taan had put all the pieces together.

Regardless, that work was a part of what he wanted to gather.

There were other things, too, of course.

Pieces of projects he'd undertaken on his own. And the Eden stuff. If the United Government wanted Torrance's head, holding onto information about the blast from Eden felt even more important. So much of Kitchell's life was in those files that he didn't think he'd feel complete if he ever lost them.

The weight of the moment fell hard on him.

He really *was* going to up and leave his life.

Until now, the idea had seemed almost farcical. Until now, he would never have thought of himself as the kind of person who could do that, but as the idea settled, he found it oddly satisfying.

He thought about clothes, and music files.

Book files and memorabilia he'd gathered throughout his entire life.

Cookware. Dishes and furniture. His bed. The idea of losing his whole living compartment and all the delightful mess he'd realized was so much a part of him suddenly came to fullness inside his mind.

What did it all mean?

The trip to his office was short — ten minutes tops.

By the time the taxi pod glided to a stop he realized he didn't have answers to any of his questions, but that the lack of answers made him somehow happier.

He got out of the taxi pod, feeling an intensity around him that he hadn't felt in a long time. The hint of dogwood came on an artificial breeze. The heat and aroma of radiating sidewalks rose from the ground. Ahead of him, the building stood — small in footprint, but built six stories tall to conserve surface area.

The taxi pod waited.

Standing there in the darkness before the Darsi building, Kitchell realized he had one more thing he needed to do.

He pulled at his dataclip.

"Message for Marisa Harthing," he said.

"Ready to receive message."

"Hi, Marisa, this is Thomas. I just wanted to let you know that there's going to be things coming out about me over the next couple of days that are going to seem ... I don't know ... um ... outlandish? They aren't going to be true — or at least the stuff the UG pushes will not be. I trust Ragnath Gavarian's work will be at least pointed in the right direction."

He paused to think about how much to add.

"I don't need you to do anything for me right now, and in fact it's probably better off if you don't. But I wanted to let you know that I'm all right, and that when I can I'll keep in touch. And I wanted you to know — if you don't already, anyway, that the UG

is taking Torrance down, so they're going to come after you, too."
He paused, considering whether he should say more.
No.
That was enough.
"Anyway. Take care. I've got to go now."
He clicked off.
"Send message now."
"Message sent."
That finished, Kitchell walked toward the building.

Chapter 43

Mars Colony Kasbian
Local Date: July 4, 2252 (Earth Standard)
Local Time: 2235

Kitchell's footsteps rang on the sidewalk.

Despite the breeze, a thin blanket of humidity seemed to cling to his skin. The building's automated security controls sensed him, and the front door slid open as he approached. He took that as a good sign — that the UG hadn't already locked down his access points.

His sensation of aloneness grew as he walked through the dark and empty corridors toward his office. At first what little lighting there was came from a series of cold blue and green luminous system lights that glowed from thermostats and other environmental controls embedded on the walls. But lighting system kicked on, and the hallway blazed with overhead lighting that flickered ahead of him as he progressed, then off behind him as he moved onward.

He came to his office.

"Open door," he said.

"Don't go in!" a voice came from down the hall.

Lights flickered on from the same direction, with the pounding of footsteps.

"Mickey?" Kitchell called.

McKinley Vivdan, a young cohort he'd done smaller projects with since arriving here, was running fast enough that his longish hair was flowing behind him. The door to the stairwell Vivdan had come from closed behind him.

"Don't go in!"

The man was close enough now that Kitchell saw his cheeks were flushed.

"What are you doing, Mickey?"

Kitchell braced himself when it became obvious that his friend was going to plow into him.

He didn't though.

Instead, Mickey grabbed Kitchell by the arm and, in stride, yanked him further down the hallway back in the direction Kitchell had come from.

Kitchell tumbled along behind Vivdan but remained upright.

"Come on!" Mickey called again.

Kitchell tried to yell that he was coming, but a pressure wave lifted him off his feet and the massive explosion from behind him drowned out any words he might have said.

He fell to the floor, skidding on his knees, and saw Mickey, too, was tumbling through the hallway.

Then everything slowed down again, and Mickey came to help Kitchell to his feet.

"Come on, Thomas," the man's lips seemed to say, though the sound barely seeped through the ringing in Kitchell's ears. *"We've got to run!"*

"What the hell?" Kitchell said as he stumbled beside his cohort.

Mickey was talking to him, but the only words that got through were "The Uglies have tried to kill you," which came just as they made the stairwell down. Emergency lights flickered on, then off, then on again, a safety warning blared, and Kitchell felt himself coming back into his body as they took the stairs.

"The Uglies?" he said.

"The United Government," Mickey replied in a quick breath. They came to the bottom of the stairs, panting. Mickey Vivdan grabbed Kitchell by the shoulders and spoke to him directly. "We really don't have time for this right now, but the basics are this: Your government wants you dead, Thomas. I'm with Universe Three, and we'd like to keep you alive. Now let's go."

Universe Three?

Kitchell noted a trickle of blood running down the side of Mickey's face, saw the wild sense of purpose in the set of Mickey's posture. His knees throbbed then. Pain began to flare where he'd landed on the meat of his left hand. Mickey gripped his upper arm and tugged with a clear sense of urgency.

Universe Three.

Mickey Vivdan was an agent for Universe Three.

The idea stuck in his brain, but nothing came out.

This time when Mickey pushed him down the hallway, though, Kitchell followed without resistance. His chest pounded as they ran down the hallway and into a back-office lab room that then connected to a service drone's doorway.

His legs began to ache, and his lungs burned with a level of exertion that he hadn't dealt with in far too long. Three steps led out of the building. He nearly turned an ankle on the last but caught himself early enough that Mickey could lead him out over the manicured lawn behind the building.

A moment later they disappeared into a row of trees, and into the humid darkness.

Behind them, flames from inside the office building licked into the nighttime.

Emergency sirens began to blare.

END GAME

NEWS

SOURCE: INFOWAVE — NEWS for the 23rd century
TRANSMITTED: July 5, 2252, Earth Standard
HEADLINE: Source Claims Ambassador Black Framed
BYLINE: Ragnath Gavarian

An anonymous informant has come forward to accuse United Government officials of framing Science Ambassador Torrance Black of conspiracy charges, likely to cover up their own involvement in the death of scientist and top Star Drive physicist Emil "Oscar" Pentabill.

The entire system was shocked when authorities found Pentabill dead while at a scientific conference, and that they considered UG Science Ambassador Torrance Black a person of interest in the case. The story became even more scandalous when reporters found proof that the United Government had information linking both Pentabill and Black to the Universe Three terrorist group.

When prosecutors released statements calling for Black's arrest, the facts seemed to be lining up. While, at first, they did not accuse Black of being an agent for U3, they would not rule that position out. They did, however, strongly suggest that Pentabill's death was an operation of Universe Three personnel against themselves.

"It's not unusual for an organization as ruthless as U3 to prune their own tree," a legal advisor to the Florecer Attorney General Attabi Kendi said. "We want to know what Torrance Black knew, and when he knew it. If Universe Three operatives knew we had his friend Oscar in our sights, there's no telling what levels they might stoop to."

The story unfolded quickly, and just days later United Government officials were building a case against Torrance Black as the assassin and accusing him of being a U3 agent himself.

Information has been found today, however, that would suggest such accusations are not true.

A contact close to Ambassador Black is reporting that UG intelligence agents have attempted to extort false reports corroborating their accusations against Black.

"The investigator threatened to accuse me of being such an agent myself if I didn't keep quiet about Torrance," the informant said. "But I can't do that to him. Torrance Black is a hero. I won't play any part in tearing him down."

The source can't confirm any particular motivation that UG officials might have to place Black in such peril, but their activity suggests that there is likely more to the situation than might ever be made public.

Chapter 44

Alexandria, Virginia
Local Date: July 5, 2252
Local Time: 2055

The sun had set only a half hour before, so it was dark on the plaza, but not so dark Zina Nichols couldn't make out the form of Willim Pinot as he strode slowly but purposely in her direction. She sat on a park bench as he came closer, listening to the nighttime around her — taxi pod doors closing, their engines silently accelerating, people moving from restaurant to bar. She wasn't hungry, but the aromas of food wafting — even from as far away as restaurant row — were intoxicating.

It was still warm in the way summertime in Alexandria can be. The air carried a coarseness, a dampness in the gentle breeze that made it feel sharp against her skin. Still, Pinot wore a hat and a business jacket that flowed down to his thighs. She couldn't make out his face in the shadows, but she knew it was him simply from the way his stride moved the mass of his body.

The director's presence carried an edge tonight, an air about him that told Zina she had no room for error. She pulled her thin jacket collar to her neck, hoping the darkness hid her nerves.

Everything Pinot controlled was done to make a point, so she understood the message behind this location.

Everguard Meadow was a monument to the historic flight, a

circular plaza laid with stone and brick, built at the center of the city. Its central focus was an iron-cast replica of the spacecraft Universe Three had destroyed. A collection of smaller monuments marked the outer ring of the plaza, each commemorating people and events critical to the UG response.

The bench she sat on while she watched Pinot's darkened form cross the open space looked inward to the central statue. Behind her rose a marble plinth with a plaque that honored Thomas Kitchell.

Pinot's breathing rasped as he stopped at the bench to survey first her and then the area around him.

"Where are they?" she said.

Pinot's body language asked her to go on.

"I understand the game, Director. You can't trust me yet, so you've got security around us. You're very good at disappearing traitors. If I make a wrong move, I suspect I'll be dead before I know it's coming. And," she said with cold modulation, "if I leave a wrong impression, there's a chance I could be dead before morning."

"Hmm," Pinot replied, removing his hat, and sitting on the end of the bench away from her. "So, what happened?"

He didn't need to specify. "I misjudged Kitchell."

"Understatement of the year."

"I'm taking care of it, though."

"Is that so?"

"You're not the only one who values insurance. I knew Kitchell talked earlier. He's being dealt with."

"Yes. I heard. Fallout?"

"None."

"Certainty on that?"

"Different approach than the original fallback plan, but same slant as the ambassador. Kitchell was moldable. Black had turned him a long time ago. Insert all the original arguments about the fact that U3 was able to avoid us here."

Pinot waited.

"Forensics will show the bomb was a type Universe Three deploys often. Magnesium fire. Burns intensely. Working concept is U3 took him out but planted the story to create a PR whirlwind that would divert attention."

"Gavarian will stand by the story."

"As they always do," Nichols said in a matter-of-fact way. "It means I'll need to burn another mole."

Pinot nodded in a way that Nichols hoped meant he approved. The loss of an agent would be difficult, but low-grade operatives were replaceable.

"Nasty business, this," Pinot said.

"We've got bigger problems, though, don't we?"

"What do you mean?"

"Mercury."

That Pinot gave no reaction surprised her.

There was a government officer aboard *Hercules*, so even if the director hadn't been consulted in advance of the jump, he had a direct line of communication there. He had to know about it. Yet his lack of response suggested a sense of self-control that she didn't think was justified. Or maybe Pinot's stoicism *was* justified. Maybe he had anticipated she would know of the event when almost no one else would. Perhaps he'd played through this scenario. Maybe his lack of reaction was a test.

"For a Grade E analyst," Pinot finally said, "you are full of such interesting news."

"Adjutant Holloway is tight with his information, Director, but I have my ways," she said both to protect Zi-Chau and to let Pinot know that she knew he knew where her information was flowing from. Pinot had to be aware of her relationship with the adjutant. It was probably why he'd agreed to mentor her to begin with.

"And what do you think of this news?"

"I think there's more there," she replied. "This isn't a simple practice of terrorism. This is an act of all-out war."

"Act of war?"

"Yes. If that's what you want to call it, anyway. I'm sure you've already asked yourself why U3 launched into Mercury's shadow. There's no strategic advantage to use it as a rendezvous or a sub-jump point. But when you string together the most germane facts, you can get an answer."

"Pentabill and Catazara," Pinot answered.

Yes, he was testing her.

Nichols felt her heart race. Until that moment, her ideas had been simple supposition that sang to her in cleaner tones than all the other suppositions put together, but the bearing of Pinot's form

as he edged forward in his bench seat, and the gravel in his voice
as he said the names cemented everything.

A sensation of warmth started at the back of her neck and
traveled down her spine.

She felt her lioness extend talons over her hip.

She was right.

This was war. Perhaps it always had been, but suddenly it had
become personal.

And though she was still young, and still inexperienced in
playing this kind of game, she'd studied enough of them to
understand that war changed the rules. React and win, think and
lose. War is chaos. Winning a war is decision.

She swallowed, then began.

"Universe Three scientists have discovered how to set a
wormhole pod," she said. "If their mission succeeded, it's likely
they've set one in our sun. So, yes. The Mercury mission means
that the United Government is now fully at war, and that there is a
real chance we have already lost."

Pinot sat fully against the bench seat, then inhaled the nighttime
air.

There was a scent of cherry blossom riding in the humidity. A
scent that was sharper as the moment dragged on. She *was* right.
She knew she was.

Pinot cleared his throat.

He stood, put his hat on his head and, with a slow movement,
arched his back to look up to where stars fought their way
through the nighttime cloud cover.

"Starting tomorrow, you will report directly to me," Pinot said.
"I'll expect you in my office at ten o'clock."

As he walked away, Zina Nichols put her hands together on her
lap and released a long breath that she hadn't realized she'd been
holding.

CHAPTER 45

Mars Colony Kasbian
Local Date: July 5, 2252 (Earth Standard)
Local Time: 0145

"I don't understand," Kitchell said when they finally arrived at a small warehouse — or to be more precise, a two-room office space inside a small warehouse. Built for a boss and an assistant, Kitchell supposed.

They'd been moving all night, hopping from an alcove to a park area, then slipping through a covered alleyway to stay for maybe two hours in an apparently abandoned apartment house that was being renovated. Now they'd come to a small production facility, which was apparently the end of the line.

It was still the darkest part of nighttime when they arrived, and the facility was otherwise empty. Still, Mickey left the lights off as they rambled up two flights of stairs to come to the office.

Even now the lighting was only a soft glow of two ten-watt LED screens angled down at the floor — covered with carpet. The lighting was enough to move safely but gave the entire place an unsettling cast of cryptic shadows.

"What is it you don't understand?" Mickey replied, slumping into a seat behind the desk and releasing a slow sigh that said he was finally relieved. His shock of long hair was straggly now. The lines on his face were thicker in the gloaming of the dim lights.

"All of it," Kitchell said, palms up and glancing around in the darkness. "The explosion. You. And now … this."

He took a seat on the large couch against the far wall.

The display above it was cold and blackened now, reflecting a hollow sheen.

Across the way the blinds were open on a small frame of windowpanes that looked out into the darkness.

"All you need to know is that the United Government wants you dead."

"And that you're from U3?"

Mickey raised his arms in supplication. "I only speak the truth."

Kitchell groaned. "Jesus. How long have you been with the enemy?"

"Seeing as we're the ones planning to save your ass, I'm not so sure you've got the right enemy in mind."

"What are you going to do to me?"

"I don't know any full plan, but I'd guess we'll jump you out of here."

"Where will I go?"

Mickey smiled. "You mean us, right? Where will *we* go?"

"I guess," Kitchell said, feeling embarrassment for reasons he couldn't say. "I'm sorry."

"I'm good as burned now, Thomas, so we'll be extracted together. And while I'm sure there are options, I'd guess we'll go straight home."

Kitchell realized what Mickey was saying. "You mean back to Universe Three's primary colony."

"Where else?"

"I don't think I can do that," Kitchell said, grimacing.

"You know you can't stay, right?"

"Yeah, but—" Kitchell stopped, staring dumbly at Mickey, and feeling a chasm in his understanding of what was going on. "Why are you here?"

The question brought more to mind.

Who had assigned Mickey this mission, and what were the circumstances that brought that about? Just how good was Universe Three's information, and where was it coming from? Was this Ragnath Gavarian's plan or something else?

"What do you know about all this?" he added.

Mickey arched an eyebrow. "Enough to save your ass."

Kitchell grimaced again. Everything was happening so fast.

"Enough to know that your UG would rather you were dead," Mickey continued. "And to say that if you don't come with us, you will be. We want you to be alive, though. And unless you want to side with the UG on this one, I need you to hang tight until we can get our assets lined up and jump you out of here."

This was the moment.

For all his professional life Thomas Kitchell had been able to avoid making this kind of decision. As a result, he could be purposefully ignorant about happenings around the world — could just do his work and not worry about anything else. But that had all changed now. He locked eyes with Mickey Vivdan and under the cloak of the office's darkness felt a sense of impending doom. All he really knew about Universe Three came from things he'd seen in the news and from the bits and pieces of their technology that he'd seen while creating technologies to defeat them. It had been easy to view them as a monolithic group of political revolutionaries who simply wanted to overthrow the United Government.

But now the events of the past few days had at least opened his eyes to ... well ... to *something*.

And now he wasn't sure what to think anymore.

Even if he wasn't going to *join* Universe Three, he realized that the choice Mickey offered was more than the organization simply taking him in as a refugee. Universe Three knew of his role. Simply the existence of Mickey as his cohort meant they understood what Kitchell had spent his life working on. They wanted him alive, but they did so only, and expressly, because of that.

If Kitchell went with Universe Three today, it wouldn't end there.

He thought about Pentabill. Thought about Torrance.

He had a decision to make, and this was the moment to make it.

"All right, Mickey," Kitchell said. "I understand."

An anxious silence hung between them as Mickey considered the comment.

The agent gave a closed-lipped nod, then pulled a device Kitchell recognized as a signal jammer from a drawer in the desk and set it on the surface with a heavy sound.

It was low-grade equipment, able to sense and absorb most commercial scanning systems.

Kitchell laughed. "You'll need a lot more than that if the UG is really chasing me."

"It's good enough to delay private bounty hunters, though, and with a little luck, that's all we'll need."

Mickey toggled power on.

Buttons on the device glowed red before flipping first to blue, then green as various levels of functionality locked in.

He paused. "You'll need to give me your dataclip, too."

"If you think I'm going to give you my personal system, you're totally insane."

"Thomas," Mickey said in a tone that made him feel like a three-year-old. He held his hand out. "Don't make me explain to perhaps the world's foremost authority on signal tracing and information processing that your dataclip is a serious liability right now."

Mickey was right.

Still, handing over his communications device felt like he was stripping bare. There were things on there that U3 could use to learn about and avoid the United Government's best opportunities to find their home system — though, admittedly it would take considerable effort to extract the information, and then extensive reengineering to fill in missing elements.

He disconnected the plug from his ear cavity and handed his cohort his device.

Mickey slid it into his pocket.

"All right," Mickey said. "Let me show you around."

He showed Kitchell the two-room office and pointed toward a lavatory closet.

"There should be something to eat in the cabinet," he said pointing to a composite cabinet with a row of drawers built into it. "I can get you reading material. No video, though. No connections. No calls." He went to the dark window and turned the horizontal blinds shut. "No access from outside, understand?"

"Understand."

"Good."

Mickey gave a terse nod, went to the door, then turned in the darkness to focus on Kitchell again. "Keep your head down and hang tight. I'll be back tomorrow with real food."

Then he was gone.

Chapter 46

Mars Colony Kasbian
Local Date: July 5, 2252
Local Time: 1615

For what must have been the hundredth time today, or was it the thousandth, Thomas Kitchell went to the window and lifted the edge of one slat.

Nothing.

Nothing beyond what he already knew, anyway, which was nothing, really.

He was in a warehouse at the edge of the community. A squat line of apartment houses stood a couple hundred paces away, and a road that ran before those apartment houses occasionally carried a taxi pod or a delivery system. A park lay behind the houses, grass green with irrigation having been a luxury thought important enough for childhood to be worth the expenditure. The angle of the slats directed his gaze such that above he could see a warp in the dome. An imperfection, really, but nothing critical.

Otherwise, the area was sleepy.

At least that meant no UG agents.

Alternatively, it meant operatives were on the hunt but were professionals who could hide in plain sight. Who the hell knew? At one point he'd seen a young woman walking a dog along the street path and he watched her intently, wondering what she was really doing and waiting to see if she'd focus on his window.

What was becoming of him?

Less than a day sitting tight in the office, and he was already going stir-crazy.

He wasn't a prisoner, but he felt caged. His brain ran loops filled with a strange combination of dread, boredom, and the unending fixation on the need to go to the window — a fight he lost more often than he wanted to admit.

Closing the blind again, he sat on the couch and tried not to think about what was going on in the world around him.

Footsteps came.

Kitchell braced against uncertainty.

A lock engaged, and Mickey stepped into the room, carrying a bag that smelled so delightful that Kitchell suddenly realized he was hungry. It was a sandwich, onions and some kind of sausage warmed together. The thermos held coffee. It wasn't much, but it beat the hell out of the dry stuff in the cabinet.

"What's going on out there?" he asked as they ate together. "What are they saying about me?"

"Better to not focus on that," Mickey said.

"Sounds like you'd best bring me a stiff drink next time," Kitchell replied.

"Best you keep your wits about you right now," came the reply — which didn't help.

They ate in silence for a bit.

For the first time, he looked closely at his cohort. Saw lines of fatigue that at one point he'd probably just chalked up to the stress of the day or a technologist's concern over some flaw in the research he was dealing with. Light from a window crack fell in a streak over Mickey Vivdan's face and down one shoulder. He was something over forty years of age but kept himself in good condition by staying in the gym every day. In the past, Kitchell just assumed he was a health nut. Now he wasn't sure.

"What's it like to live like this?" Kitchell asked.

"Live like what?"

"To be always ready to leave the life you've built at the drop of a moment?"

"This *is* my life, Thomas," Mickey replied with something that might have been bravado. "I don't feel like I'm *leaving* anything."

"I see," he said, though he didn't.

He thought about Mickey as he chewed a bite of his sandwich. Why did Kitchell trust him?

Because — yes — despite knowing so little about him, Kitchell did, indeed, trust Mickey Vivdan.

How much do we really know about other people?

"What's that?"

Kitchell chuffed. "Nothing," he said, swallowing. "Just thinking out loud."

Talking to himself was something he'd done in the past, but he was alone so often it didn't matter. He'd have to be more careful in the future.

"I don't think I can do this," Kitchell said. He cupped his head into his hands, then rubbed his fists back over his eyes.

"I don't think you have a choice."

Kitchell looked up at Mickey. "There's always a choice."

"Fair enough," Mickey said. He paused, though. "Things are moving, Thomas. Hang tight and you'll get your answers soon. Between you and me, though, I think the real question you need to be asking yourself is why your government is trying to blow you to stardust."

Kitchell gave an exasperated chuff. "That's a complicated question."

"I'm sure it is. But it's the only one that matters."

Then Mickey left the room and shut the door behind him.

Kitchell didn't have anything to do but cycle over the admonition that he should "keep your wits about you right now." The words, along with the intensity of Mickey's expression when he'd said them, kept Kitchell on a tripwire of alertness.

It didn't help that the factory was busy below his office, and that daytime noises rang out in random fashion, each clang and yelp bringing him to full alert, each lull in the operation driving him to peer once again out the window.

After another full day, he was so wired that when Mickey arrived with dinner, he nearly wept.

Nighttime was even worse.

Joints popped and pinged as the building contracted in the coolness of the night. Automated maintenance routines clicked and whirled on and off. Cleaning agents activated.

It was a never-ending cacophony of sound that made Kitchell jump at every fresh start.

Being unable to sleep beyond fits and starts gave him even more time to think about Universe Three.

Still, he had no answers.

He knew systemwide politics was a messy game even when he was trying to avoid it, but everything seemed even more jumbled when he tried to focus on it. He was going to have to take a stand someplace, though. Sometime soon. He just wasn't sure where that someplace should be, or exactly how soon that sometime would be.

Universe Three would certainly work to debrief him.

How far would they go?

He'd seen their tech often enough to know their scientists were good. What could he share without giving too much away? Or should he even care to shield anything?

What would they do if he didn't give them what they wanted?

What were they going to do with him?

Could he join them?

The idea sat like a rock in his gut, but given what the UGIO was doing to him, were U3 agents any different?

Pacing around the dark carpet, he thought about Torrance.

Once Kitchell asked Mickey if he had any news about LC, but Vivdan said he didn't.

A thought struck him with such clarity he knew it had to be the truth, though.

"The UGIO is working to have Torrance tagged as a U3 agent," he said, thinking out loud. "And then make him take the fall for killing Oscar." A chill crossed his spine as he made a turn. He recalled the investigator's demeanor.

"They're doing the same thing to me. It'll be a domino chain," he said. "They're going to say Universe Three killed me."

He stopped pacing. "Mickey. That's who they'll blame for my disappearance. With Mickey gone, too, he'll be easy to weave into a spy story of epic proportions."

The idea made Kitchell laugh. At least they'd be right about Mickey Vivdan, anyway.

"Blind squirrels and acorns," he muttered.

He thought about Marisa. Where was she in all this? Was her

position inside the Interstellar Command being questioned? He wanted to talk to her, but the idea was farcical now.

Yes.

Systemwide politics was messy and complex.

On the third night Mickey finally woke him up.

"Get your things together," he said, shaking Kitchell's shoulder. "It's time."

CHAPTER 47

Mars Colony Kasbian
Local Date: July 7, 2252 (Earth Standard)
Local Time: 2305

After slipping out of the office, Thomas Kitchell and Mickey Vivdan clambered into the cramped compartment of a private taxi pod, which then took off. The enclosed compartment was quiet. It smelled of plastic and dry air.

The ride was smooth, but days in seclusion had tuned Kitchell's ears to everything around him. He heard the drive engines whine, the gentle hiss of friction as air flowed against the cockpit, and the occasional click of a relay or control adjustment firing.

The display was set on a map that Kitchell could follow.

"Jagger's Field?"

He'd been there often.

It was a central hub with properly built exit locks to support a wide variety of flights into and out of the domed colony — both interplanetary junkets and hops into low orbit.

"Seems kind of public, doesn't it?"

"Public flights are best for getting off the ground in a hurry," Mickey said.

Kitchell furrowed his brows.

"UG monitors every flight," Mickey explained. "So, things can get hairy quick if something takes off without a plan. We're going to board a training skimmer that's already authorized to run a training plan. Lessons, you know?" He shook his head with a dour frown. "The problem is that I'm incorrigibly unable to be taught."

Then Mickey gave a shrug that made Kitchell laugh.

Truth was he'd always liked Mickey for his sense of humor, and now that it was coming out again it made Kitchell feel more relaxed — if Mickey was loosening up, perhaps it meant things were going to go well.

"Once we're in the upper ranges of the atmosphere, we'll make a quick diversion from plan. At that point it should be too late to stop us."

Kitchell gave his own ironic smile. "Should be?"

"Yeah. The timing has to be right, but it's the safest way to get in and get out."

"I've got a lot to learn about the spy game."

"Don't worry, though. We've done it before on other evacs at other fields. We've got solid coordinates. The challenge will be getting you on the skimmer."

"Just what I needed to hear."

Mickey's smile was wide this time.

Minutes later they arrived at a hangar.

"Pull your collar up," Mickey said, following his own advice.

"Will that help?"

Another smile came. "Probably not, but it makes it more fun, doesn't it?"

Then the doors popped open, and they were on the tarmac.

Beside them, on a fully prepped launch pad, sat a fully fueled private skimmer. A brief jaunt from the taxi pod, and their footsteps echoed in the enclosed entryway as they came aboard.

Mickey took the pilot seat, and motioned Kitchell to copilot's. The door shut behind them with a solid sound. Mechanisms whined.

Confused, Kitchell took the seat. He'd expected a pilot.

"I thought you couldn't be taught?"

"You haven't seen me fly yet."

Mickey checked the controls, leading Kitchell to do the same, his mind swooning with an element of despair. He'd flown skimmers in college, but that was really the last time. Now the multiple rows of system controllers, guidance arrays, and engine commands seemed like so much soup.

Mickey seemed fine, though, running through a brief set of checks.

With one last glance at Kitchell, Mickey Vivdan opened the channel.

"Control Command, this is skimmer tail C7E6 requesting air space under flight plan C7E6 number one. Please inform when we're authorized for departure."

Despite Mickey's controlled voice, Kitchell found himself holding his breath.

What if they didn't receive authorization?

Would they take off anyway?

He understood protocol meant the controller would let them through anyway — as precaution against suicide sabotage if nothing else, but then they'd almost surely be easy prey for the colony's law enforcement wings. And if UG was on high alert, as Kitchell expected they would be, it boded even worse.

He hoped Mickey was an experienced flyer.

"C7E6, this is Control Command. Authorization for departure is granted."

Concentration covered Mickey's face as he guided the craft to final launch status. A minute later they were flying.

The field display showed other craft in the area.

UG craft?

Kitchell couldn't help but think about it.

They seemed so close now, so close to being gone.

The three days of anxiety he'd just been through gathered into a single flare of excruciating intensity that pounded in his temple.

A lock door built into the dome above them opened as they approached.

The skimmer nosed harder up, pushing Kitchell into his seat. None of the craft on the display seemed to be doing anything unusual. The lock shut behind them as they made proper altitude, and a magnetic field booster helped them gain speed as the vacuum pumps embedded in the airspace between the lock doors suctioned atmosphere away.

The final air lock opened before them, and Mickey hit the booster trims.

The skimmer rumbled and rattled but settled as they made it to the thin air of Mars's upper atmosphere. Finally, Mickey throttled down.

Friction was gone.

Kitchell felt the truly joyous sensation that was zero-g.

"We made it!" he screamed.

"Not quite yet," Mickey said, though he too was beaming.

Then a spaceship appeared in space. A Star Drive so close Kitchell thought they might ram it. The word *Defender* was stenciled into the lower rim at the spacecraft's bow.

His heart pumped, and in that moment everything became real.

He knew Universe Three ships.

He understood what it meant.

A stream of chatter between the controller and Mickey filled the cockpit, but Kitchell's gaze was on the curve of the ship's hull and the way its engines were laid out. It was a thing of beauty, really — the whole idea of space flight. He'd forgotten that over the years. Forgotten how amazing the entire concept of space flight had been to human beings even a mere couple hundred years before.

He split his time, then: watching Mickey bring the skimmer into the docking bay that opened in *Defender*'s hold, but also watching stars glimmering in the distance.

Then the skimmer entered *Defender*'s loading bay and gave a final lurch as it locked down on a receiving pad.

"Prepare for jump," a voice came over the radio.

"Hold tight," Mickey said.

Kitchell glanced over the stark control panels. "Wish we could see the lights," he said.

Mickey shrugged. "Maybe next time."

A few moments later: *"Jump procedure complete. Stand down systems."*

It was over.

As they exited the skimmer, Thomas Kitchell knew the Universe Three Star Drive spacecraft had already jumped.

Chapter 48

Apogee: 37 Gem System
Local Date: C13/D1
Local Time: 1/10:15

Deidra Francis stepped into the briefing room to find Commander Mikayla and the retrieved agent, McKinley Vivdan, already seated. It had been a busy morning already, having started well before normal hours — which was fine by her. She hadn't been able to sleep anyway.

She was still angry from the loss of *Vengeance.*

Still hadn't had time to fully process it.

Time for grief would come as it would, though. Until then, there was work to do.

The black hole gate was set. Her staff had plans to make.

Even though the drain was slower than Catazara had predicted, the gaping maw of a singularity was now siphoning the sun that powered the UG and its Solar System. It meant their own plans could proceed. Expansion into new colonies was on the table.

Her morning had been spent visiting wounded members of the *Vengeance* mission, but her afternoon would be focused on the future.

"Good to see you again, Jess," she said to the commander.

"You also, Director."

Despite having so recently jumped, Deidra had decided to use

Defender for the extraction mission specifically as a reward for Jessamine Mikayla.

Thomas Kitchell, the UG scientist this whole thing was about, was seated at the table, too — across from Mikayla and Vivdan. His head was down, and he had placed his hands in his lap in such a way as she could see restraints over his wrists.

She'd read the reports — knew details about the UG op he'd found himself caught up in. She knew more about Thomas Kitchell, too. She'd long paid attention to him simply because of the core elements of his work were critical to UG's attempts to find them, and — in fact — had once considered authorizing an operation to extract him earlier. But when first informed of Kitchell's current situation, Deidra had asked for every piece of information they had on the scientist. So refreshed, she knew more about Thomas Kitchell than anyone else in the room — perhaps including Kitchell himself.

Now, she wondered how far he'd come in this process, how far he had bent in their direction, and how much farther he was willing to go.

Captain Shudar, who had technically led *Defender*'s extraction jump, was also there, standing at a refreshment dispenser and collecting a tray of drinks.

"Where is Martin?" she said as the door shut behind her.

"Communications Leader Scalese has just gotten off his skimmer," the captain said as he put the tray on the table. The aroma of stout coffee followed. "He'll be here momentarily."

"Excellent."

Deidra took a padded seat.

"I don't think those cuffs are necessary, are they?" she said to Kitchell.

"No," he replied.

"Mr. Vivdan?" Deidra said, indicating the spy should remove the shackles.

The agent was a wild card here.

Vivdan's reports were good, but Deidra hadn't worked directly with him. He'd been a mole in sleep mode for over a standard decade, always diligent, and clearly able to withstand that kind of pressure. Would he respond well to being removed from the field? She didn't know, but she'd seen things go different ways.

Right now, however, she was more worried about whether Vivdan had prepared Kitchell well enough.

"Thank you," Kitchell said a moment later, absently rubbing his wrists.

The door snapped open and Scalese entered the room.

"Let me introduce you to Martin Scalese," Deidra said. "Martin leads our communications and intelligence operation."

Kitchell nodded.

"Do you know why you are here?" Deidra asked.

"I'm not sure I know what to think about anything anymore, to be honest," the scientist replied.

Deidra wrapped her hands around a mug.

"That's a difference between us, Thomas," she said. "I know what to think about a lot of things. I think, for example, that you are a ranking member of a group of people who have been working for a very long time to find and destroy my people. And I think you've gotten closer to succeeding than any of us in the room would prefer to believe."

Kitchell's glance went to Vivdan's.

"What do you want to know?" Kitchell said.

"Let's start with how close UG is to finding us."

"I don't know."

Deidra leveled her gaze at him. "I'm sensing a problem here."

"I know the algorithms," Kitchell snapped back. "And I know the signal profiles we're looking for. But to tell you how long it will take for those algorithms to succeed requires that I know where you are to begin with."

Deidra nodded. "You are a dangerous person, Thomas. You know that, don't you?"

"I have no idea what that means," Kitchell said.

"I'm a dangerous person, too," Deidra said, ignoring him. "And I am a dangerous person who is willing to do whatever it takes to save my people. You *are* dangerous. But you are also smart. So let me state this directly: I want you to work with Mr. Scalese here, and between the two of you I want you to arrive at a solution that will throw your United Government off our tracks for as long as possible. Do you think you can do that?"

Kitchell looked at her then, and the answer seemed to click fully into place.

"Yes," he said. "I can do that."

"Good," Deidra said.

She stood up to leave then and waited for Kitchell's gaze to track back to hers. When their eyes locked, she saw his fragile state.

She made a decision then.

Staring him in the face, she thought Kitchell seemed a reasonable man. A man who might come fully to them if given the proper motivation. Even if he didn't, Kitchell had a sense of honor to him that felt authentic. If so, he deserved the truth — or at least *a* truth — which is something she had to give.

"You've been under a great deal of stress, Thomas," she said. "That you are still cogent speaks well of you."

"Thank you," Kitchell said.

"I have news you may be interested in."

"News?"

"Information," she said. "About Torrance Black."

EPILOGUES

Thomas

Apogee: 37 Gem System
Local Date: C13/D1
Local Time: 1/10:25

"Information about Torrance Black."

The words were a punch to the gut.

"How do you know about Torrance?"

She waited.

"Is he alive?"

Deidra Francis took a silent breath. "He was transferred to one of our Star Drive spacecraft after the Florecer fiasco. But that ship is no more."

Kitchell let the information flow over him.

Torrance had been on a U3 spaceship.

"Was he with you?"

"You mean, was he a spy?"

Kitchell nodded.

"No," Deidra Francis said. "Torrance Black was never an agent for us. He got caught up in one of our games, though. He was on *Icarus* because it was the only way we could collect him."

Kitchell let his stare fall to the table.

He nodded absently, unable to get up the energy it would take to scoff. "That's it then," he said. "We are all just pawns in your games."

"A person is only a pawn if they choose to ignore the game they are playing," she replied. "So, no. Torrance Black was not a pawn. He didn't know a game was even being played."

Kitchell felt a new truth in the director's words. He experienced the idea behind the director's words better than he understood them. Which was fine. It was a soundbite, not a definition — and whatever profundity Deidra Francis thought might be embedded in the comment didn't change the fact that Torrance Black was dead.

Still, though, Kitchell felt the comment gather in his chest, felt the truth burning inside it settle through his body.

A person is only a pawn if they choose to be, he thought.

Only a pawn if they see the truth and decide not to do anything about it.

Otherwise, they — like Torrance had been, and like Kitchell had been — were not even in the game.

They were simply fodder.

He thought that was right.

Kitchell looked at Deidra Francis, then. Took in the depth of her gaze and the lines on her face. He'd felt the aura of power that radiated from the Universe Three director the moment she'd walked into the command room.

He knew of her, of course. Her reputation, anyway.

She was bloodthirsty.

And she was sharp.

A master tactician, even better than her father before her. And, yes, she was dangerous — a word he had been thinking about just as she assigned that tag to him. She was not above taking any action that would weaken the United Government. Now he watched her take him in — scanning him as if seeing something deep inside him — and he wasn't sure what to think.

In Deidra Francis's gaze, Thomas Kitchell saw a truth about himself, though.

He had spent his adult life avoiding certain realities around him, seeing them but pretending they didn't exist even as he was contributing to them.

Now he had seen the layer of ugliness that lay under the UG framework. Now he understood a truth about them, and therefore about himself.

He was glad he'd come to the decision to work with the U3 intelligence office before meeting with her because otherwise he might have felt coerced.

Instead, he simply felt hollow. He was tired, and suddenly drained. His body felt unable to respond.

But he understood it was time he changed his ways.

Did that mean joining Universe Three?

Maybe. Maybe not. Power corrupts, he thought.

He'd work with U3 now because it felt like the right thing to do, but he wouldn't trust them any more than he would the United Government.

Either way, he was never again going to be fodder.

"Thank you for telling me that," he finally said.

"You're welcome," she said.

Deidra Francis, Director of Universe Three, left the command room.

Kitchell drew a breath big enough to stretch his ribs, then looked at Martin Scalese.

"Well," he said. "I guess it's time we got started."

DEIDRA

Apogee: 37 Gem System
Local Date: C13/D3
Local Time: 2/4:10

Sitting alone in her office, feeling the early morning air flowing in from the open wall, Deidra Francis turned her attention to Kazima Yamada's plans. With the black hole gate set, the United Government would eventually be forced to leave them alone — or at least divert attention from their search for considerable time. With Thomas Kitchell providing a layer of safeguard in that area, Deidra felt as secure as she'd felt since their departure from Atropos.

Outside, the sky was growing light as their home star neared the horizon. Sounds of the city picked up volume.

She scanned the plans again.

Yamada was proposing to split the community, building three new colonies on nearby planets.

"Separate cities means losing one would not destroy the movement," Yamada had said at their last staff session.

It wasn't a controversial idea — cleaving the community — but it was one fraught with emotion, and one that if not executed well could cause serious setbacks.

While Yamada's thinking would leave them less open to attack as well as give them new resource pools to draw from, it would also mean separating families and taking the risks that came with every such expedition. U3's population was large enough to accept most of those risks, but in this case, it would also likely mean that their combined manufacturing capacity would have to be deployed to build equipment and housing needed for this kind of construction rather than focusing on building more Star Drive spacecraft.

For a while, anyway.

For Deidra that was a feature rather than a bug.

She thought about her father, and about Gregor Anderson. About all the people in the Universe Three movement who had given so much. The community was preparing for another memorial, this time to those lost on *Vengeance*. She thought about the pilots who had saved the lives of both her and Allie Feder. About the security leader who had escorted them to the shuttle bay, and who had lost his life to those first blasts.

Keth Enid was the man's name.

She hadn't known anything about the young man but had felt a need to look it up when they got home. He'd just turned twenty.

A faction of her staff would argue for the need of more Star Drive craft — Captain Keyes, who had been retrieved in the rescue effort, carrying the most weight.

She considered the whole of the battle for Mercury.

Thinking of everything that went right, and everything that went wrong. Thinking about how the results of so many battles throughout history rested on so many random events and so many decisions made by people who never received their due.

Jessamine Mikayla, for example.

It would be Gregor Anderson who would go down in U3 lore as the man who changed the course of history, but it was Commander Mikayla who had made the fateful decision to give her command to Gregor when she knew she didn't have to, and it was Jessamine Mikayla who carried out the mission when Gregor was lost.

McKinley Vivdan, too.

He was like hundreds of other agents Universe Three had scattered in UG territory, risking their lives every day simply by existing.

Deidra scratched her chin, trying unsuccessfully to focus.

Universe Three was here because of so many people.

So, yes, it was time to focus resources on those people who remained.

While such expansion would be hard medicine, Deidra Francis and the rest of Universe Three's leadership had learned from the past. Putting all their people in one place was a path to disaster.

The 37 Gem system held three additional habitable planets and several others with resources that could be mined. Though transportation and supply logistics still needed to be developed to ensure everyone had resources they needed, Yamada and Kyleen Lian — the biotech specialist who managed agriculture and farming — and her team would do it, though. Yamada's plans showed how Apogee and each of the three new cities would support each other, focusing on proximity to water, fertile land, and shelter first, then allowing the communities to grow into their industrial purposes as quickly as their organics allowed.

It was time, she thought.

It was time.

As she thought of these cities of the future, she let herself dwell one more time on the past.

I'll call them Rosa, Talia, and Kel Melody, Deidra thought.

Rosa and Talia for Katriana Martinez's two daughters, and Kel Melody for the love of Deidra's life.

As she thought of those three names, Apogee's home star rose high enough to crest the mountain range and a beam of light fell across her face.

Yes, she thought, *I'll call them Rosa, Talia, and Kel Melody.*

ALLIE

Apogee: 37 Gem System
Local Date: C13/D12
Local Time: 2/13:15

It was late when Allie Feder stepped out of her small compartment and walked out to the central patio she shared with the neighborhood. Darkness was thick here. No lights, but stars for as far as she could see. It was "quiet," too, the community sleeping to prepare for another day of construction, another day of progress.

Insects gave a steady music, the red-winged crickets so prevalent on the planet.

Something the biologists said was a combination of a lizard and a frog added a low bellow of a bass to the song.

She sat on a lounge chair and laid her head back, letting out the sigh of a breath, trying to relax.

Catazara had asked her to take the lead on their project to discover why the black hole gate wasn't yielding as quickly as he'd projected. They wanted a better answer to the question of how long the Solar System had to live.

The equations were troubling her to the extent she couldn't sleep.

Something else ate at her stomach, too, though she hadn't told anyone.

"I thought I might find you here."

Allie jumped, and her hand went to her pounding heart.

She turned to find Deidra Francis behind her.

"I'm sorry to startle you," the director said.

"Oh, it's fine, Director."

"Deidra. I thought we had established that already."

Allie smiled. "I'm sorry. Deidra."

"I couldn't sleep either," the director said.

Deidra came farther around the patio plaza. She had a bottle with her. Wine, Allie saw. The director raised it. "Do you mind if I sit with you?"

Allie motioned to the chair beside her.

"You're always welcome at my place," she said. "Especially if you come armed with hooch."

Deidra sat and held the bottle to her.

Allie took it. Its weight said it was nearly full. She sipped.

"Blend," she said. "I like that."

The wine here tasted sharper than wines she remembered from Atropos.

"Yeah," Deidra answered. "I find pure wines here too tart."

Allie stifled a laugh.

She felt close to Deidra in a way she couldn't really define. The director was older than her — almost old enough to be her mother, really. But there was something about Deidra Francis that made Allie comfortable.

She took another swallow, then handed the wine back to the director.

"It's hard, isn't it?" Deidra said, tipping the bottle.

"What do you mean?"

"To be responsible for things this big."

Allie drew in a breath, and for a moment — as the world around her melted into a sensation so big she couldn't describe — fought the need to cry.

"Yes," she said, looking at Deidra in the darkness. "It is hard."

The director had said as much earlier, but Allie hadn't fully gathered it in, but now — with Apogee's insects and lizard-frogs serenading her, and with Catazara's project filling her mind — she felt it.

Deidra Francis understood her.

"They still have time," Deidra said.

"I've heard all the justifications," Allie replied, dismissing her with a wave of her hand.

She'd heard the arguments.

Even if the black hole gate was draining the sun as quickly as Catazara had originally projected, the Solar System had time to react. Decades, possibly. Enough time to create colonies in systems that the UG had already visited, especially if they acted now.

It was a lot of lives, though.

A lot of lives that depended on the United Government doing the right things.

History was not on those people's side.

Deidra drank again.

The bottle sloshed gently as she handed it to Allie.

"Genie's out of the bottle," Deidra said. "And there's no putting it back. But you did the right thing, Allie. I want you to know that."

Allie shrugged and ran math inside her head.

"It's a hundred billion people. Give or take. And they don't make all the decisions."

"That's why it's hard," Deidra said.

Allie took a drink of wine.

Deidra had done her best to remove pressure from Allie's shoulders, had even taken the burden of making the command that set the gate. If there was anyone on the planet who understood how Allie felt, it would have to be Deidra Francis. But not even Deidra could truly see the depths of her being right now. The technology to set remote gates existed due to her work. So, regardless of who pulled the trigger, the simple fact that a black hole gate existed to begin with was due to Allie Feder.

Her gaze went into the black sky.

The day had been cloudless, the nighttime no different.

Stars twinkled.

Her gaze went to one, fifty-seven light years away and just rising over the horizon, barely perceptible to her naked eye.

"I hope you're right," she said.

ZINA

Crystal City, Virginia
Local Date: July 7, 2252
Local Time: 1855

Zina Nichols was not surprised to find an empty bed when she arrived at their apartment. Zi-Chau hadn't come home last night, either, so the empty bed tonight carried a stronger note. It said Zi-Chau Holloway wasn't ever coming home.

The idea settled as she shouldered her bag onto the couch, went to the food processor, and ordered it to make a plate of noodles and gravy.

She was going to miss his cooking.

His empty seat sat before the table.

She supposed she should feel guilty. Exposing him as the source of her information had been a gamble she'd needed to take, and Pinot closed the leak. But it was the right move all around. She felt the truth of that as a boldness of the moment, in the way sound from the food processor built into a savory melody. The aroma of that food, cooking, felt like certainty. She would have done the same thing if she were in the director's chair — and, as such, it served as a test of Pinot in the same way the director had been constantly assessing her.

That Zi-Chau was so lackadaisical was not her fault, but she was required to understand that laziness was a trait that permeated a person. If he was that loose around her, he would be the same elsewhere.

The system chimed to say dinner was ready.

Zina felt warmth from the ceramic dish as she went to the table and began to eat.

It was good, she thought. Good enough, anyway. The gravy was comforting.

A last glance at the empty chair across from her cemented the moment.

That Zi-Chau Holloway was no longer alive meant Pinot, too, understood Zi-Chau had been a soft man in a soft job, and soft men in soft jobs are dangerous. It meant that Pinot, too, understood how certain truths shift when at war.

It said something else, too.

She would need to be careful.

That Pinot could make an adjutant to an admiral of the UG Chief of Staff disappear without any trace said that her boss was even more powerful than she had guessed. Her first days as his direct report proved that Pinot was still suspicious of her.

That was fine, though.

He was wise to be so.

The upper echelons of the UG government were still fighting to hold onto their devastating secret about a new link in the sun, arguing about what it meant, and trying to position themselves for whatever fallout was going to come from it. It wasn't something that could stay secret for long, though. Science is science. Truth eventually becomes certain. But it meant there would be new games to play — games with ultimate consequences.

Zina Nichols had been thinking about those games, though.

She had ideas.

She smiled then, despite herself, as she finished her noodles, and sopped up the last of the gravy.

Yes, she would most certainly miss Zi-Chau's cooking.

This is the end of

STARGAMES

STEALING THE SUN: BOOK 7

If you enjoyed this story, you might be interested in the rest of the series:

STARFLIGHT

STARBURST

STARFALL

STARCLASH

STARBOUND

STARCRASH

STARGAMES

STARDUST

STARBORN

If you enjoyed this story, please consider stopping by your favorite online booksellers' websites and leaving a review. Word of mouth is the most powerful force in the universe when it comes to the livelihood of your favorite authors.

ACKNOWLEDGMENTS

I would like to thank my first readers, Sharon Bass and John Bodin, for being able to see what I'm trying to do and help me get there. I also want to thank the entire community of creative people who run around in my sphere of existence. You each make me feel unworthy, yet at the same time inspire me to do my best.

I would like to thank my wife and amazing copy editor Lisa. I can promise you any errors in these pages were created after they passed through her hands.

I would like to thank my daughter Brigid, too, both for being one of those amazingly talented creatives I mentioned a moment ago (you should most definitely read her work), and for being so helpful as I've made my way through this last daunting year or two.

And, finally, I would like to thank you — the reader of this — for supporting my work.

It is greatly appreciated.

ABOUT THE AUTHOR

Ron Collins is an Amazon best-selling Dark Fantasy author who writes across the spectrum of fiction genres.

His fantasy series *Saga of the God-Touched Mage* reached #1 on Amazon's bestselling dark fantasy list in the UK and #2 in the US. His short story "The White Game" was nominated for the Short Mystery Fiction Society's Derringer Award.

He has contributed a hundred or so short stories to *Analog*, *Asimov's*, Fiction River Anthology Series, and several other professional magazines and anthologies.

He holds a degree in Mechanical Engineering, and has worked to develop avionics systems, electronics, and information technology before chucking it all to write full-time — which he now does from his home in the shadows of the Santa Catalina Mountains.

Ron's website is: www.typosphere.com
Follow Ron on Twitter: @roncollins13

Sign up for his newsletter to get free stuff!

http://www.typosphere.com/newsletter